DOC SAVAGE'S AMAZING CREW

William Harper Littlejohn, the bespectacled scientist who was the world's greatest living expert on geology and archaeology.

Colonel John Renwick, "Renny," his favorite sport was pounding his massive fists through heavy, paneled doors.

Lieutenant Colonel Andrew Blodgett Mayfair, "Monk," only a few inches over five feet tall, and yet over 260 pounds. His brutish exterior concealed the mind of a great scientist.

Major Thomas J. Roberts, "Long Tom," was the physical weakling of the crowd, but a genius at electricity.

Brigadier General Theodore Marley Brooks, slender and waspy, he was never without his ominous, black, sword cane.

TOGETHER WITH THEIR LEADER, THEY WOULD GO ANYWHERE, FIGHT ANYONE, DARE EVERYTHING—SEEKING EXCITEMENT AND PERILOUS ADVENTURE!

Books by Kenneth Robeson

🦅 Published by Bantam Books

BRAND OF THE WEREWOLF

A DOC SAVAGE ADVENTURE

by Kenneth Robeson

BANTAM BOOKS · TORONTO · NEW YORK · LONDON

BRAND OF THE WEREWOLF
*A Bantam Book / published by arrangement with
The Condé Nast Publications Inc.*

PRINTING HISTORY
Originally published in DOC SAVAGE *Magazine January 1934*
Bantam edition published April 1965
2nd printing

*Bantam Books are published by Bantam Books, Inc., a subsidiary
of Grosset & Dunlap, Inc. Its trade-mark, consisting of the words
"Bantam Books" and the portrayal of a bantam, is registered in the
United States Patent Office and in other countries. Marca Registrada.
Bantam Books, Inc., 271 Madison Avenue, New York, N. Y. 10016.*

PRINTED IN THE UNITED STATES OF AMERICA

BRAND OF THE WEREWOLF

Chapter 1

THE STRANGE MESSAGE

It was a little way station on the transcontinental railroad in western Canada. Only one man worked there. He had what railroaders call an "OS" job. About all he had to do was "OS" trains—telegraph the dispatcher that they were passing his point.

Usually, nothing much ever happened around there.

Just now, however, the telegrapher looked as if things were happening—big things. His manner was as excited as that of a small boy about to see the circus.

The thing which had flustered him was a telegram that he had just copied. It was addressed to a passenger on the fast express train which was due to arrive soon.

The operator interrupted his routine work frequently to stare at the name of the individual to whom the message was going. He scratched his head.

"If that man is the fellow I think he is—" He finished his remark with a low whistle of amazement.

Some minutes later, the brass pounder gave a start as if he had just thought of something. He got up hastily and went to a row of shelves in the rear of the room. These held magazines. Due to the loneliness of his post, the operator was a heavy reader.

He picked out and thumbed through several magazines which made a practice of publishing stories of famous men. The cover design of one of these consisted of a large bronze-colored question mark. Printed across this were the words:

THE MAN OF MYSTERY
(Story on page 9)

The telegrapher opened the magazine to page nine. The story was what writers call a "fact article." Every word was supposed to be the truth. More large black type asked:

WHO IS PROBABLY THE MOST AMAZING OF LIVING MEN?

The telegraph operator had read this story before. But now he started to peruse it again. He was interrupted.

A train whistled in the distance, and soon its approaching roar was soon audible.

It was the fast passenger. Smoke and steam rolling, air brakes shrieking, the engine and string of coaches came to a halt. A regular stop for water was made here.

Wilkie came in. Wilkie was the conductor. He had a large head, and an extraordinarily prominent stomach. He looked like a pleasant little goblin in a uniform.

"Hyah, brass mauler!" he greeted cheerfully.

With a dramatic gesture, the operator passed over the telegram.

"Message for one of the passengers, eh?" said Wilkie, and started to stuff the missive in a pocket.

"Wait a minute!" ejaculated the telegrapher. "Look who that's for!"

Wilkie eyed the name on the telegram.

"For the love of Mike!" he exclaimed.

"I knew you'd heard of him," the operator said triumphantly.

Wilkie absently removed the uniform cap from his enormous head. "Do you reckon this is the same man?"

"I'm betting it is," said the telegrapher. "He's taking a vacation—him and the five men who help him. He has a relative up in the woods along the coast. He's paying a visit there."

"How do you know that?" Wilkie demanded.

The operator grinned. "It's kinda lonesome here, and I kill time by listening to the messages that go back and forth over the wires. I heard the message he sent, saying he was coming with his five friends."

Wilkie hesitated, then read the message. As an employee of the company, he probably had a right to do this.

"Whew!" he exclaimed. "If that chap was a relative of mine, I wouldn't send him a telegram like this!"

"Me either!" the operator replied. He secured the magazine which he had started to read. "Say, did you see the article in here about that fellow?"

Wilkie glanced at the magazine. "Nope. I'd like to read it, too."

"Take it." The operator passed the magazine over. "It's sure worth reading. It tells some of the things he and his five men have done. I tell you, Wilkie, a lot of the things are hard to believe. This fellow must be a superman!"

"Them writers sometimes exaggerate," Wilkie said.

"Not in this magazine," the telegrapher assured him. "It's got a reputation of sticking close to the truth."

The engine whistle moaned out. Echoes came slamming back from the timbered hills.

"That's the ol' highball!" Wilkie wheeled. "Thanks for the magazine. Be seeing you, brass pounder."

The train was moving. With a smoothness that came of long practice, Wilkie swung aboard. He headed for the cars which held drawing-rooms. He walked the swaying aisles with the proficiency of a sailor on a rolling deck of a storm-tossed ship.

Opening the magazine at page nine, he stared at the article. The first paragraph gripped him. Absorbed in his reading, he nearly fell over a suitcase which some traveler had left protruding into the aisle.

"What a man!" Wilkie ejaculated.

The traveler who owned the suitcase, mistakenly thinking the remark was directed at himself, looked indignant.

Wilkie reached the drawing-rooms, and found the porter. "I'm hunting for this man," he said, and showed the name on the telegram.

"Yassah!" gulped the porter. "Golly me! Dat's de stranges'-lookin' man Ah evah saw!"

"What's strange about him?"

"Man, he am de bigges' fella yo' evah laid yo' eyes on!" The porter gazed ecstatically ceilingward. "When he looks at yo', yo' jus' kinda turns inside out. Ah seed him with his shirt off, takin' some kinda exercises. Ah nevah seed such muscles befo'. Dey was like big ropes tied around him."

Wilkie nodded. He had come on duty at the last division point, and had not seen all the passengers. "In the observation car, eh? And I'll know him when I see him?"

"Yo' cain't miss him! He's a great big bronze man!"

Wilkie headed for the observation car.

Back in the tiny way station, the telegraph sounder was clicking noisily. The operator sat down at his typewriter to receive.

He copied the incoming message number, the office of origin, and the address. The missive was destined for a passenger on another train.

The telegrapher reached over to his key and "broke."

"Wrong number," he transmitted.

Telegrams were numbered in consecutive order. This was to prevent a telegrapher sending one "into the air"—transmitting a message which was not received at the other end.

"It's the right number," the man at the distant key tapped.

"You're shy a number," explained the station wireman. "You sent me a message half an hour ago."

"The last message we sent you was four hours ago," rattled the sounder.

The telegrapher shook his head in bewilderment. Getting out his carbon copy of the message which he had given to Wilkie, he "traced" it to the distant man—outlining its contents.

"We sent no such message," he was informed.

"I received it," the station operator clicked back. "There's something strange about this. Do you think the wires were tapped?"

"Search me."

The telegrapher sat and pondered. He reached a decision. Grasping the key, he transmitted: "I'm going to wire ahead to the next station, and let Wilkie know what happened."

"Why go to all that trouble?" the distant operator demanded.

"Because both Wilkie and I thought the contents of that message were strange. We both remarked that it was an unusual communication for this man to receive."

"What do you know about the business of the man the message was going to?"

"I've read of the fellow," tapped the station operator. "I'll tell you about him later. He's worth hearing about. But I'm going to wire Wilkie now."

He began to maul out the call letters of a station at which Wilkie's train would soon arrive.

The station door opened furtively behind him. It made no noise. Two men crept in. They were clad in grease-spattered coveralls. Both had handkerchiefs tied over their faces, and both carried revolvers.

The telegrapher, absorbed in calling, did not hear them. It was doubtful if he ever knew of their presence.

One of the marauders jammed his revolver to the operator's temple, and pulled the trigger. The report of the shot was deafening.

The operator tumbled from his chair. He had died instantly.

Reaching over, the murderer grasped the telegraph key.

"Never mind that stuff about another message," he transmitted. "I was mistaken."

"That lonesome place must be driving you nuts," chided the distant telegrapher, thinking he was still talking to the station man.

The killer gave an ugly laugh. He grabbed the key again.

"Nuts, nuts! Ha, ha, ha!" he transmitted erratically. "King George couldn't be crazy. Ha, ha! I'm King George——"

For several minutes he sent crazily, in the manner of a

demented man. Then he carefully wiped the finger prints off the murder revolver and placed it in the fingers of the lifeless station telegrapher.

"That fixes it up," he told his companion. "They'll think he went mad and committed suicide. Nobody can trace my gun. The numbers are filed off."

"I don't like this!" gulped the fellow's companion.

"We hadda keep 'em from findin' out we tapped the wire and sent that message, didn't we? C'mon! Let's blow!"

The pair departed. Some time later, a somber black monoplane lifted them from a level bit of grassland which lay about three miles from the tiny station.

The plane moaned off in the eye of the evening sun. It was following the railroad westward, as if in pursuit of the passenger train.

Wilkie, the conductor, stood stock-still in the observation car and stared. The colored porter's words, and what he had read of the article in the magazine, had prepared him to a degree for what he was seeing. Yet the personage before him was even more remarkable than he had expected.

Had Wilkie not known better, he would have sworn the individual was a statue sculptured from solid bronze. The effect of the metallic figure was amazing.

The man's unusually high forehead, the muscular and strong mouth, the lean and corded cheeks, denoted a rare power of character. The bronze hair was a shade darker than the bronze skin. It lay straight and smooth.

Only by comparing the bronze man's size to that of the observation car chair in which he sat, were his gigantic proportions evident. The bulk of his great frame was lost in its perfect symmetry. No part of the man seemed overdeveloped.

Wilkie snapped himself out of his trance and advanced.

"Doc Savage?" he asked.

The bronze man glanced up.

Wilkie suddenly realized the most striking thing about the fellow was his eyes. They were like pools of flake gold glistening in the afternoon sunlight that reflected through the train windows. Their gaze possessed an almost hypnotic quality, a strange ability to literally convey the owner's desires with their glance.

Undeniably, here was an amazing man.

"Doc Savage," he said. "That is right."

The man's voice impressed Wilkie as being very much in keeping with his appearance. It was vibrant with controlled power.

"A wire came for you at the last station," said Wilkie, and handed over the message. It was the first time in years that Wilkie had been awed in the presence of anybody.

"Thank you," said Doc Savage.

Wilkie found himself retreating, although he had intended to hang around and strike up a conversation with this remarkable man. The tone of those two words had impelled him to depart. At the same time, he found himself feeling very friendly toward the metallic giant.

It was eerie, the things the bronze man's voice could do.

Wilkie was almost out of the observation car when another weird thing happened. An uncanny sound reached his ears.

He came to an abrupt stop. His face was blank. Absently, he felt of his ears. The sound was so curious that he half suspected it might be a product of his imagination. The note seemed to be coming from no particular spot, but from everywhere.

It was low, mellow, and trilling, that sound—like the song of some strange feathered denizen of the jungle, or the sound of a wind crawling through a leafless wilderness. It ran up and down the musical scale, having no tune, yet melodious. Then it ended.

Wilkie did not feel awed by the sound. Rather, there was something inspiring about it.

As he went on, Wilkie felt as if he had just taken a drink of fine old liquor. The trilling sound had that kind of an effect.

Chapter 2

THE TRAIN WEREWOLF

The sound Wilkie had heard was part of Doc Savage. It was a small, unconscious thing which he did in moments of intense concentration, or when he was surprised. Often when Doc made the sound, he was unaware of doing so.

Reading the text of the telegram had caused the tiny, weird note to come into being.

Leaving his chair, Doc strode for the observation platform on the rear of the coach.

There were other passengers. These were amazed by the bronze man's appearance—so much so that they forgot their manners and frankly stared.

A stout, elderly man with a slightly swarthy face gazed at

the bronze giant's hands. Enormous, supple tendons showed those hands contained incredible strength. The hands seemed to mesmerize the swarthy man.

A ravishingly pretty dark-haired girl sat beside the elderly man. Her eyes were large and limpid, and her lips a most inviting rosebud. She looked very fresh and crisp, so impeccable, in fact, that it was obvious she had not been on the train long. Even the neatest of individuals soon show the effects of traveling.

These two were clearly father and daughter.

The attractive young woman seemed intrigued, not by the bronze man's undeniable physical strength, but by the fact that he was one of the handsomest fellows she had ever seen.

Doc Savage went on, seeming not to notice the pair.

Frowning, the elderly man dropped a hand on his daughter's arm.

"Quita allá!" he ejaculated severely in Spanish. "For shame! You were smiling at that man, Cere."

The enchanting Cere colored in confusion. She *had* smiled, although she had not meant to.

"Eso es espantoso!" she laughed. "It is dreadful! Thank goodness, he did not see me. He would have thought me very forward."

"Si, si," her parent agreed disapprovingly.

Father and daughter were staring after the receding bronze man when a low voice sounded at their side.

A man had joined them silently. This individual was tall and slenderly athletic. His face was more than handsome. It was pretty. It was almost a girl's face. His age was somewhere around thirty-five. He had hard eyes.

"I trust you are retaining your courage, señorita," he said fawningly. He bowed to her father. "You also, Señor Corto Oveja."

"You need have no fear of our nerve, El Rabanos," said Cere in excellent English. "Instead of discussing our troubles, we were remarking on the striking qualities of the bronze man who just passed. Do you happen to know his name?"

The girl-faced El Rabanos leaned close to breathe: "Not so loud, señorita!"

A close observer could have noted that the pretty señorita had suddenly begun turning pale. "You mean——"

"The bronze man is Doc Savage," said El Rabanos.

Señor Corto Oveja came up rigid in his chair. "So that is the man—the fiend who is to kill us! *Dios mio!*"

"Si, si!" muttered El Rabanos. "We must watch this Doc Savage. From him, our very lives are in danger."

"And his appearance made such a good impression," Cere murmured forlornly.

Doc Savage, unaware of the bombshell his passage had exploded, stepped out on the observation platform.

One man rode there. The outstanding thing about this fellow was his gigantic hands. Each of these was composed of more than a quart of bone and gristle, sheathed in hide that resembled rusted sheet iron. The man was very big— over six feet, and weighing fully two hundred and fifty pounds—but the size of his hands made the rest of him seem dwarfed.

He had a long, Puritanical face, which bore an expression of great gloom. He looked like a man on his way to a funeral.

"Have a look, Renny," said Doc Savage, and extended the telegram.

The big-fisted man was Colonel John Renwick, known in many parts of the globe for his accomplishments as an engineer. Also, he was noted for a playful habit of knocking panels out of doors with his incredible fists. With either fist, he boasted, he could vanquish the stoutest wooden door.

Renny's funeral-going expression was the one he habitually wore when at peace with the world.

Renny was one of a group of five singular men who were Doc Savage's helpers.

The telegram was addressed to Doc Savage, care of the train, and read:

JUST RECEIVED YOUR WIRE ADVISING YOU ARE PAYING ME A VISIT STOP WISH TO INFORM YOU I HAVE NO USE FOR REST OF SAVAGE FAMILY STOP DO NOT WISH YOUR COMPANY STOP WOULD BE DELIGHTED TO HAVE YOU STAY AWAY   ALEX SAVAGE

Renny had a pet expression which he used on all occasions calling for vehemence. He employed it now.

"Holy cow!" he exploded.

"Those are something near my own sentiments," Doc Savage agreed.

"Dang it!" Renny's voice was something like the roaring of an angry animal in a cave. "What if he don't want our company? The crowd of us weren't going to drop in and sponge off him! We were going to do some fishing and hunting, and merely pay him a visit as a courtesy. If he don't want us, we won't bother him. But I'll be blasted if that will keep us from our vacation!"

"Alex Savage owns a large stretch of land along the coast," Doc pointed out. "It has the reputation of being the best spot in Canada for hunting and fishing."

Renny groaned thunderously. "A fine gesture of welcome! Say, Doc, don't this Alex Savage know you?"

"Not personally," Doc replied. "He is an uncle. I have never met either him or his daughter."

"Daughter?"

"An only child, I understand. Her name is Patricia. Age about eighteen."

Renny tapped his huge fists together. This made a sound remindful of two flint boulders colliding with each other.

"If your uncle and cousin don't want us, Doc, I reckon we'll go somewhere else," he said gloomily. "Where's the map? I'll try to find another place where there's good fishing."

"Better postpone that, Renny," Doc said dryly.

"Huh?"

"There's something very suspicious about this message," Doc Savage informed him.

Puzzled and wondering, big-fisted Renny followed his giant bronze chief back through the observation car. Renny's relation to Doc Savage was unusual. He willingly carried out Doc's smallest order. Yet Renny received not one penny of salary.

Renny, in fact, was considerably more than a millionaire in his own right. His skill as an engineer had made him a fortune. He had, in a sense, retired—retired to follow the trail of what he liked above all else, adventure. Peril and excitement were the spice of his life.

Peril, excitement, and adventure were the bonds which cemented him to Doc Savage. Doc seemed always to walk amid these things. Each minute of his life was one of danger.

For Doc Savage had a strange purpose in life, a creed to which his existence was dedicated. That creed was to go here and there, to the far corners of the earth, helping those in need of help, punishing those who needed punishment.

Doc had been trained for this purpose from the cradle.

The other four aides of the bronze man, like Renny, were bound to him by a love of adventure. And, like Renny, they were masters of some profession.

One was an electrical wizard, one a world-renowned chemist, another a great geologist and archæologist, and the fourth, one of the most astute lawyers Harvard had ever turned out.

Trouble-busting was the life purpose of Doc and his five aides. Their exploits had pushed their fame to the ends of the earth. Doc, mighty man of bronze, was by way of becoming a legend—a specter of terror where evil-doers were concerned.

Doc Savage entered his drawing-room, Renny at his heels. The room was stacked with bags and many metal boxes equipped with carrying straps.

Doc opened one of the boxes. A compact radio transmitter and receiver came to light. Corded fingers moving with deftness, Doc manipulated the controls. The set was fitted with a "bug"—a mechanical key for rapid transmission.

"What station are you callin', Doc?" Renny queried.

"There is a Royal Canadian Mounted Police station in the railroad town nearest Alex Savage's home," Doc explained. "I'm trying to raise them."

Renny heard this without batting an eye. That Doc should know there was a Mounted station at the town, and have the call letters at his finger tips, did not impress Renny as anything out of the ordinary. Doc Savage had a fabulous fund of information of all kinds.

Doc contacted the Mounted station, and made known his identity.

"At your service, Mr. Savage," was the reply to this.

Renny heard this come from the ear phones. He was not surprised. This was not the only great police system which coöperated fully with Doc Savage.

"I received a telegram which pretends to have been sent from your town by Alex Savage," Doc transmitted. "Will you check up and see if it was sent, please?"

There followed fully five minutes of silence, while the distant Mounted operator made inquiries.

"No such message was sent from here," came back the report.

Doc wirelessed his thanks, then replaced the radio set in its case.

"You've got one guess about that telegram," he told Renny.

"It was a fake!" Renny thumped. "But, Doc, what in blazes made you suspicious?"

"The message was addressed care of this train," Doc explained. "Our earlier message to Alex Savage said nothing about what train we would be on."

Doc Savage, Renny lumbering at his side, now sought out Wilkie, the conductor.

Wilkie was absorbed in the magazine which held the feature story about Doc Savage.

"How soon will we reach a point from which I can send a telegram?" Doc inquired.

Wilkie swallowed twice before he could answer. What he had been reading had tended to increase his awe of this bronze man.

"We pass a little station in a few minutes," he replied. "We don't stop, but I can clip it to an order hoop, and get it to the telegrapher as we go past."

"Good!"

Doc proceeded to write out a message. It was addressed to Alex Savage:

SOMETHING STRANGE GOING ON STOP DID YOU GET MY TELEGRAM ADVISING THAT MYSELF AND FIVE FRIENDS PLANNING SPEND FISHING AND HUNTING VACATION YOUR VICINITY STOP DID YOU WIRE US NOT TO COME STOP PLEASE ADVISE IMMEDIATELY

DOC SAVAGE

Folding this, Doc gave it to the conductor.

"I don't know what it will cost," Wilkie said.

"This should more than cover it." Doc passed over a large Canadian five-dollar bill. "Keep the change for your trouble."

"I couldn't do that," Wilkie said hastily. "I'll deadhead the message for you, Mr. Savage. It won't cost a thing."

Wilkie was outdoing himself to please the bronze man.

Doc seemed faintly puzzled for a moment. Then he caught sight of the magazine article which Wilkie had been reading. His inscrutable, metallic features did not change, but after a moment he indicated the periodical.

"The chap who wrote that had a lot of imagination," he said dryly.

Doc and Renny turned away from the admiring conductor. They almost bumped into two swarthy men and a beautiful, dark-haired girl. These were Señor Corto Oveja, his daughter Cere, and the girl-faced El Rabanos.

The three looked steadily away from Doc and Renny. They had been standing there eavesdropping as Doc gave Wilkie his message. But they did not want the bronze giant to know that.

Doc and Renny went on up the car.

"A peach!" Renny breathed when they were in the next car.

"What?" said Doc.

"The girl with those two swarthy men," Renny murmured. "Holy cow! Was she a looker!"

"You mean the three who were spying on us as we gave the conductor that message?" Doc queried softly.

Renny gulped: "They were spying on us?"

"They were."

Señor Corto Oveja, Cere, and El Rabanos would have been surprised, had they overheard this statement. They had not imagined they had been discovered. They did not know that few things happening around Doc escaped his attention.

Renny scowled and banged his knuckles together. "What do you make of this, Doc?"

"Somebody wants to keep us away from Alex Savage's place, and the beautiful señorita and her two dark-complexioned companions are very interested in us," Doc summarized.

"But what's at the bottom of it?"

"Trouble!"

"You're tellin' me?" Renny grimaced. "But what's at the bottom of it?"

"I neglected to bring my crystal ball," Doc said dryly.

Renny grinned. Somebody, incredulous at the eerie precision with which Doc could read the meaning of mysterious events, and deduct what was to come, had once declared the bronze man was a mystic, able to see the future in a crystal ball. The truth was that Doc's foresight came from a brain that operated with crystal clarity.

"The rest of the gang will want to know about this," Renny suggested.

Renny was referring to the other four members of Doc's little group. These gentlemen were playing a game of chess in another drawing-room.

"A good idea," Doc agreed. "We'll tell them."

Doc and Renny went to a drawing-room door. Doc's hand, drifting toward the knob, came to a rigid stop.

"Look!" He pointed at the door.

The panel bore a weirdly shaped smudge. Faintly imprinted, discernible only after a close glance, the thing was more than a foot high, and about half as wide.

Renny stepped around so that he got a better view with the light on it.

"Holy cow!" he gasped. "The thing is shaped like a wolf head, Doc—a wolf with hideous, humanlike features!"

Doc nodded slowly. His bronze lineaments, his strange golden eyes, had not changed expression.

"Werewolf," he said.

"What?" Renny was puzzled. "There ain't no such critter. It's just a legend of these Canadian trappers and natives."

"A legend of human beings who, thirsting for the blood of their fellow men, turn into wolves that they may satisfy their vampire lust," Doc said quietly. "Most unsavory creatures, even for ghost stories."

Renny hesitated, then stroked a finger through the design on the door. His enormous digit left a clean path in its wake.

"Just dust!" he muttered. "But it's strange it'd settle there in that kind of a shape."

Doc tried the door. It resisted. He showed no surprise. "Locked," he said.

"Blazes! Something's wrong!" Without hesitating, Renny blocked one huge hand into a fist. He swung it.

The door panel was of metal, but it gave as if it were a kicked tin can. With a loud crack, the lock broke. The panel jumped open.

Doc and Renny shouldered in.

Four men lay sprawled about a table. Their positions were grotesque; they lay exactly as they had fallen from their chairs.

The men were Doc Savage's four aides.

"They're dead!" Renny wailed.

At that instant, a small depot flashed by the speeding train. It was the station at which Wilkie planned to drop Doc Savage's telegram.

Wilkie got rid of the message successfully, and before the train was out of sight, he saw the station telegrapher, carrying the missive, enter his office.

Chapter 3

WARNING OF THE WEREWOLF

The window of the drawing-room in which the four rigid forms lay, was closed tightly. Lunging to it, Doc wrenched up the sliding sash. The noise of the train wheels came in through the window like the moaning of a mechanical monster.

Big-fisted Renny, after his one wailing cry that the four men were dead, went into action. He sank beside one of the prone forms.

The individual over whom Renny stooped was a startling

figure. He hardly exceeded five feet in height, yet outweighed Renny's own tremendous bulk fully ten pounds. Nearly as wide as he was tall, he had arms inches longer than his legs. His face was incredibly homely. The fellow who would pass as first cousin to a gorilla.

This was "Monk." As Lieutenant Colonel Andrew Blodgett Mayfair, his accomplishments in the field of experimental chemistry were known to both hemispheres.

"Holy cow!" Renny yelled. "They're not dead!"

Doc Savage replied nothing. He made a round of the drawing-room, sensitive nostrils testing the air. His weird, flake-pool golden eyes roved about.

He examined the doorlock, the key. The latter was in place from the inside. Obviously, the drawing-room had been locked from the interior.

Doc picked up the nearest of his four inert friends. This man was extremely tall, and as thin as a skeleton. His coat draped on his shoulders as on a coat hanger. Spectacles were still in place on his nose. These were peculiar, in that the left lens was extraordinarily thick.

This man was "Johnny"—William Harper Littlejohn. The proudest possession of a famous Eastern museum was an archæological exhibit of the ancient Mayan civilization which Johnny had contributed. Mining engineers consulted textbooks which he had written on geology.

Johnny had lost use of his left eye in the War. Needing a magnifying glass in his business, he carried one in the left side of his spectacles for convenience.

Doc Savage hurried into the corridor. Within a few minutes he was back, carrying a medical case.

He began administering restoratives.

"Pulse very slow in all four of them," he announced to Renny. "Respiration only perceptible when you hold a mirror in front of their lips. They're about all in."

"Ain't a mark on 'em!" Renny rumbled.

"So I notice," Doc agreed.

"But what happened to them?"

"Something very mysterious," Doc said grimly. "Let's snap them out of it and see if they can shed light on what has occurred."

Strangely enough, it was the most unhealthy-looking fellow in the group who was first to revive. To all appearances, this man was easily the weakling of the crowd. He was undersized, slender, only fairly set up, with a none too healthy complexion. He had pale hair and pale eyes. He looked as if he might have lived most of his life in a dark and mouldy cellar.

This was "Long Tom" Roberts. Long Tom—he was occasionally known as Major Thomas J. Roberts—was an electrical expert. "A wizard of the juice!"—men of his own profession declared.

Long Tom frowned blankly at the table, on which a chessboard stood. Then he peered at his three motionless fellows.

"What kind of a game are those guys playing?" he demanded weakly.

"Game, hell!" Renny boomed. "Listen, Long Tom, we busted in here and found you four birds all spread out. What happened?"

Long Tom considered. "I don't know."

"You don't——" Renny waved his huge hands. "Come on! Snap out of it!"

"We went to sleep," Long Tom groaned. "We just felt drowsy all of a sudden, then went to sleep."

"You have no idea what caused it?" Doc questioned.

"Nope."

Doc continued his resuscitation efforts on the other men.

"Ham" was the second individual to awaken. Ham was famed for two things: he was one of the cleverest lawyers Harvard had ever turned out, and he was a snappy dresser. Tailors often followed Brigadier General Theodore Marley Brooks down the street, to see clothes being worn as they should be worn. He was a slender man, quick moving, and a fast thinker.

It chanced that, as Ham's eyes opened, the first figure he saw was homely, gorillalike Monk.

"I can't be in heaven!" he grinned feebly.

Renny snorted. Ham was always making some wisecrack at Monk's expense. To listen to the sharp-tongued lawyer, one would think nothing would have given him more delight than to see Monk burned at the stake.

This peeve of Ham's dated back to the Great War—to an event which had earned him his nickname. Thinking to have fun, Ham had taught Monk some French words which were highly insulting, telling him they were the proper expressions with which to flatter a Frenchman. Monk had addressed the words to a French general, and landed in the guardhouse.

But very shortly after Monk's release, Ham was hailed up on a charge of stealing hams. He was convicted; somebody had planted the evidence. Ham was mortally certain Monk had framed him. But to this day, he had not been able to prove it.

"What happened to you guys?" Renny asked.

Ham acquired a bewildered expression. He moved about weakly until his hands found a black cane. This cane appeared innocent-looking. Actually, housed in its slender length, was a razor-sharp sword. The tip of this blade was daubed with a chemical, a touch of which, in a wound, would produce instant unconsciousness. Ham was rarely seen without his sword cane.

"He don't know what happened to him!" Renny boomed, interpreting Ham's befuddled expression.

Johnny, the archæologist and geologist, and the homely Monk now opened their eyes. Johnny promptly felt for his glasses which had the magnifying lens, just as Ham had groped for his sword cane.

Both men admitted they had not the slightest idea of what had happened. While playing chess, they had simply gone to sleep.

Monk had a small, childlike voice that was surprisingly mild for one of his apish build.

"Well, what about the head of the werewolf on the door outside?" Doc asked them.

Puzzled wonderment stamped the faces of the four men. Doc knew they had no knowledge of the weird design on the door.

"A werewolf!" Monk muttered.

"I just called it that," Doc told him. "It is the head of a wolf, with a grotesquely human face."

Bracing himself on his sword cane, Ham sought to sit erect. He gave it up and fell back dizzily.

"Golly, I feel washed up!" he groaned.

"Ain't that too bad!" Monk jeered faintly.

Ham ignored the insult. "I can't imagine what is behind it, Doc. We were just sitting here———"

His eyes protruded. His hands grasped his sword cane wrathfully.

Under the bed, an unearthly squealing and grunting suddenly arose.

"Habeas Corpus!" Monk yelled weakly, but joyfully.

A pig staggered from under the bed. The porker family probably never produced a more grotesque specimen than this one. The pig had legs as long as those of a dog, and ears that rivaled airplane wings.

"Ow-w-w!" Ham groaned.

Habeas Corpus was the present great misery of Ham's existence. Monk had bought the pig on a recent expedition to

Arabia, paying the equivalent of four cents in American money as purchase price for him.

Monk's story was that Habeas Corpus's former owner, an Arab, had sold the pig because he had been making a nuisance of himself by catching hyenas and dragging their carcasses up to the house. It was possible that either Monk or the Arab had exaggerated.

The homely Monk was greatly attached to Habeas Corpus, probably because the presence of the pig enraged Ham.

"The door was locked on the inside, and you had the windows closed?" Doc inquired.

"That's right," Ham replied.

"The pig seemed to have been laid out, the same as you fellows," Doc said dryly. "It's all very mystifying. This isn't the first queer thing that's happened, either."

Ham blinked. "What do you mean?"

Doc told them about the telegram incident.

"Do you think the fake telegram and what happened to us has a connection?" Ham demanded.

"Can't say," Doc replied.

Doc went to a hand bag and opened it. The piece of baggage held several weapons which resembled overgrown automatic pistols. They were fitted with curled magazines.

These were machine guns of Doc's own invention. The weapons were tiny, compared to the destruction they could wreak. They fired so rapidly that their roar was like the note of a gigantic bull-fiddle. Magazines were charged with what big-game hunters call "mercy bullets"—slugs which produce unconsciousness instead of death.

Doc distributed the rapid-firers to the four weakened victims of the mystery attack.

"Keep a sharp lookout!" he warned.

Renny demanded: "What are you gonna do, Doc?"

"You and I are going to talk to the three persons who were eavesdropping when I gave the conductor the telegram," Doc told him.

Trailed by Renny, Doc glided out into the corridor.

The two men had not progressed far when they encountered Wilkie.

"I'd like to get some information about two dark-complexioned men on the train," Doc told the conductor.

Wilkie scratched his large head. "There are a number of dark men aboard, I notice."

At this, Renny shot a sharp glance at Doc. The bronze man's features told nothing.

"The two I am interested in were in the company of a very pretty girl," Doc explained.

"Oh, them!" grinned Wilkie. "They got on at the division point where I went on duty. That was two stops back."

"Know their names?"

"No. Passengers don't usually give a conductor their names."

"Have you noticed anything queer about their actions?" Doc persisted.

Wilkie scratched his large head again. "Nothing, except that they seem to be moving around a lot."

"These swarthy men—did they get on at the same time?" Wilkie nodded. "Yes. At the division point."

Doc and Renny left the goblinlike little conductor.

"This thing is beginning to shape up like a mess of first-class trouble," Renny said thoughtfully.

Doc said nothing. He sought and found a porter.

The porter directed him to a drawing-room which had been reserved by the three individuals whom Doc wished to see.

Doc found the door and knocked. Silence answered. He rippled his knuckles on the panel again. Then he tried the knob. The door was locked.

Doc called the porter. "You're sure they're in here?"

"Yas, suh," said the porter. "Dey went in about five minutes ago. Two of 'em did, anyhow—dat pretty gal and her papa. Don't know if dat man with de gal face is in dere or not."

Renny held up a huge fist and gave Doc an inquiring look. "I guess we'll go in," Doc told him.

Renny drew back to slam his fist against the panel. Then he lurched. The train had slackened speed abruptly. Renny had to grasp the doorknob to maintain his balance.

"Guess we're pulling into a station," he rumbled.

Bang! went his big fist against the door. The sheet metal bulged, but held. Renny swung again terrifically. It seemed a miracle that his fist was not smashed to a pulp.

The train had slowed rapidly; it was now crawling.

Renny's next punch exploded the door open. He plunged across the threshold, then brought up quickly, his jaw asag.

"Holy cow!" he gulped.

Señor Corto Oveja and his attractive daughter were draped across the drawing-room bed. They lay perfectly still. Black leather straps were drawn so tightly around their necks as to be almost buried in the flesh!

Chapter 4

DEAD MAN

"The window!" ejaculated rock-fisted Renny. "It's open!"

"Take a look!" Doc rapped. "Whoever did this may have jumped out as the train slowed down."

Doc was already bending over the two forms on the bed. The garroting straps were strong, yet they broke under Doc's sinewy fingers like cardboard strips.

The girl's wrist in one hand, the man's in the other, Doc explored for pulse.

Both were still alive; pulse was strong, respiration firm.

"This didn't happen more than a few moments ago," Doc told Renny. "The would-be killers must have escaped through the window."

Renny, his head thrust outside, boomed: "I don't see anybody!"

"They had time to duck."

"Yeah," Renny agreed. He lifted his gaze skyward. "Holy cow! That thing is almost an omen!"

"What is?"

"An airplane flying overhead!" Renny rumbled. "The thing is black—looks kinda like a buzzard."

Doc stepped to the window and studied the plane. His sharp eye noted something Renny had missed.

"That plane has no identification numeral!" he said sharply.

Renny made a silent whistle. "In view of what's happening on this train, that's more than passing strange, eh? Planes on lawful business usually have identification numbers."

Like a somber vulture, the black monoplane dipped off to the westward, and was soon lost to sight.

Doc twisted a faucet at the washbowl, caught cold water in a palm, carried it over and dashed it on the faces of Señor Corto Oveja and his daughter. He waited expectantly, but they did not stir.

"They should be coming out of it!" Doc said in a vaguely puzzled tone.

He tested pulse and respiration. Then, for the briefest moment, the bronze man's weird trilling note was audible. It trailed softly up and down the musical scale, and abruptly was gone.

Turning to Renny, Doc said: "It looks as if, in addition to being choked, they got a dose of the same thing our four friends got—that weird unconsciousness."

Renny was staring fixedly at the door. There was an expression of bewilderment on his long, puritanical face.

"Yeah," he mumbled. "Look, Doc!"

His huge hand indicated the inner side of the door panel which he had damaged.

The sheet metal bore an eerie smudge. It had the likeness of a wolf head—a wolf with horribly human features.

"I saw it earlier," Doc explained.

"You did!" Renny gulped. He had not seen Doc show any surprise, whenever it was that he had made the discovery.

"That same mark was on the other door," Doc Savage said. He stepped close to the hideous smear. His eyes measured it. "It's exactly the same size, too."

Renny nodded. He could not tell, himself, that this mark was the same size as the other. He knew Doc Savage could judge the relative sizes within fractions of an inch.

"Two men have been accompanying this girl about," Renny rumbled. "I wonder where the other one is."

With a rather unpleasant jerk, the train got into motion.

"We'll revive this man and the girl," Doc declared. "Then we'll hunt the other one."

"Yeah!" Renny boomed. "We'll get that gink!"

Outside in the passage, a man yelled shrilly. "Help! Help! They're going to kill me!"

Renny and Doc bounded to the door. They expected to see a murder scene—or at least a fight. They got a shock.

The swarthy, girl-faced man stood in the corridor. He leveled an arm at Doc and Renny.

"You heard them!" he bellowed. "They said they would *get* me. *Sabe!* That means they plan to kill me!"

Wilkie, the conductor, stood just behind the girl-faced man. Wilkie looked flabbergasted.

"Now, now, mister," Wilkie said soothingly. "There's some mistake here."

"It is no mistake!" wailed the dark man. "Look quickly! They must have killed my friends, Señor and Señorita Oveja!"

Wilkie advanced. He mumbled apologetically to Doc: "I sure don't know what this is all about."

The swarthy man yelled: "I know what it's all about, señor! This bronze man is trying to kill my friends and myself."

He came to the door and looked in. *"Eo es terrible!* It is terrible! What did I tell you? They are murderers!"

Renny made big square blocks of his fists. "You'd better dry up, girl-face!"

At this point, Señor Corto Oveja and his daughter showed

signs of reviving. Doc splashed more water on them. They stirred about, and finally opened their eyes.

Señor Oveja pointed weakly at Doc.

"Seize that caballero!" he cried feebly. "It was he who attacked us."

Renny was perfectly familiar with Doc's ability to control his emotions. Yet, watching the bronze man now, he had to marvel; Doc showed by not the remotest sign that anything out of the ordinary had occurred.

"You," Doc said, "are mistaken!"

"It is true!" Señor Oveja shrieked weakly.

"*Si, si!*" echoed his pretty daughter. "This man Savage is the one who assaulted us. We became strangely drowsy as we sat here in our room. Before complete unconsciousness overcame us, men entered and began tying straps around our necks. One of them addressed the other as Señor Savage."

"Did he say *Señor* Savage?" Doc asked pointedly.

The girl shut her eyes. Apparently she was thinking. "Yes. He used the word 'señor.' "

Doc glanced at Renny.

The big-fisted engineer was staring at the leather straps which had been around the necks of Señor Oveja and the girl, choking them to death. From the expression on his somber face, he might have been looking at a pair of poisonous serpents.

"I thought you'd notice those straps," Doc told him quietly. "They're carrying-straps from a piece of my luggage."

The man with the womanish face bellowed triumphantly: "*Bueno!* This proves it beyond a shadow of a doubt. Savage tried to do murder! Conductor, arrest him!"

Wilkie shifted from one foot to the other. Little bubbles of perspiration stood on his large forehead. He made a bewildered gesture.

"What is your name?" he asked the girl-faced man.

"El Rabanos," the fellow replied.

"What is the motive?" Wilkie demanded. "Why should Doc Savage try to kill you?"

El Rabanos hesitated. A strange expression flickered about his eyes.

"I don't know," he said finally.

Wilkie scowled. "Did you think previously that you were in danger from Doc Savage?"

"Yes," El Rabanos admitted reluctantly.

"For what reason?" Wilkie cracked back.

El Rabanos said angrily: "You arrest this man! Turn him over to the Mounted Police. I'll give them my full story."

Wilkie eyed Doc. "I don't want to arrest you, Mr. Savage,

but I may have to. Something strange and horrible is going on around here. I wouldn't be surprised if the death of that poor telegraph operator hasn't got something to do with it."

"What telegraph operator?" Doc queried sharply.

"The fellow who copied the message that I gave you," Wilkie explained.

Once more Doc Savage received surprising information without an appreciable show of emotion. Doc was not callous. He simply had his nerves under such control that they behaved as he wished.

"Was the telegrapher murdered?" he queried.

"Not according to a report I got at our last stop," Wilkie replied. "A section worker found the body. He claimed it looked like suicide. But I knew that operator. He wasn't the kind to take his own life."

Doc's hand described a gesture which took in Señor Oveja, his daughter, and El Rabanos.

"I should like very much to hear these three explain why they fear me," he said.

All Doc received was a hateful stare from each of the trio. The girl's look was the least malicious. In fact, her expression portrayed rather plainly that she regretted that this handsome bronze man was an enemy.

"It don't seem like they're gonna talk," Wilkie muttered.

Doc Savage swung over to the door. He closed it so that the rear of the panel was visible, and indicated the smear which resembled a grisly, human-faced wolf.

"Maybe you can explain this!" His powerful voice crashed.

The girl's eyes flew wide as she saw the smudge. She screamed with a sort of exhausted horror. Then she clamped palms over her eyes.

Señor Oveja and El Rabanos reacted almost as sharply. Their eyes protruded; their jaws fell.

"The werewolf!" choked Señor Oveja.

"What does it mean?" Doc questioned.

Pretty Señorita Oveja laughed hysterically. "Why should you be asking us? You know very well what it means!"

"You three are under some misapprehension," Doc told them. "This is all a mystery to me."

"Que!" El Rabanos ejaculated sarcastically. "What! Did not your uncle Alex Savage take you into his confidence?"

"So Alex Savage is mixed up in this," Doc said dryly.

"Mixed is a very mild word for it, Señor Savage," El Rabanos sneered.

Ignoring the girl-faced man, Doc Savage turned to Wilkie.

"One of the gang who assaulted Señor Oveja and his daughter called the other by the name of *Señor* Savage. Obviously they were trying to frame me. But use of the Spanish word 'señor' was a slip. I believe you said there were other swarthy-skinned men on this train."

"Right!" exclaimed Wilkie. "I'm going to check up on them right now."

The goblinlike little conductor hurried off.

Doc paid a visit to his four friends who had been victims of the weird sleep. There was no danger of any one escaping from the speeding train.

When he entered the drawing-room, Monk and Ham were scowling blackly at each other. This was a good sign. It indicated Monk and Ham were back to their normal quarreling state.

Johnny and Long Tom also seemed fairly chipper.

"The effects of the stuff wear off quickly," said gaunt Johnny, polishing his spectacles which had the magnifying left lens. "What's new, Doc?"

"We're in the thick of a mess," Doc announced.

Instead of looking gloomy or apprehensive at this, all four men grinned. They were a strange bunch. Peril and excitement were the things for which they lived.

Speaking rapidly, Doc told them what had happened when he went to investigate Señor Oveja, the daughter, and El Rabanos.

"They seem to think I'm some kind of a bogy man," he finished.

"Do they really think that, or are they pretending?" questioned apish Monk, scratching the airplane-wing ears of his pig, Habeas Corpus.

"I'm not sure yet," Doc replied.

The train whistle moaned. Its sound was a banshee wail over the noisy progress of the coaches.

Doc glanced through the window. It was only a road crossing for which the train had whistled.

A porter ran past the drawing-room door, crying in a horror-stricken voice: "Lawsy me! Lawsy me!"

Doc collared him. "What is it?" he demanded of the porter.

"It am de conductor, Mistah Wilkie," the colored man moaned.

"What about him?"

"He done been stuck!"

"Show me where he is!" Doc commanded.

Wilkie lay in the washroom of a Pullman car—lay in a wet lake of crimson which had leaked from his own body. He had been knifed numerous times in the chest.

Doc Savage was skilled in many things—but in surgery and medicine above all others. A glance convinced him that Wilkie was dead.

"Anybody see anything?" Doc asked the porter.

"No sah!" said the porter. "Not that Ah knows of."

Doc Savage stood like an image graven in the metal he resembled.

On the washroom door, he had discovered another of the hideous smears—a human-faced wolf. The mark of death!

Standing there, the bronze man was so quiet as to seem without life. An unseen monster of horror and death was slowly wreathing its tentacles about him. Why, he did not know. But it must be something that concerned his uncle, Alex Savage, or his uncle's daughter, Patricia.

Absently, Doc's golden eyes roved to the north and west. In that direction lay the estate of Alex Savage. And there, it was possible, lay also the explanation of the mystery.

Chapter 5

THE WEREWOLF CRIES

Doc Savage was a man of profound accomplishments. But he was no clairvoyant with a gift of transporting his vision. So he was unaware that mystery and horror also stalked the domain of Alex Savage.

There, too, the werewolf was spreading its uncanny violence.

The estate of Alex Savage was no mere backwoods homestead. It was true that forty years ago Alex Savage had homesteaded it. But now it had grown, until the estate spanned up and down the coast for miles, and reached no little distance inland.

Scattered over other parts of Canada, Alex Savage had wheat ranches, mines, and an industrial plant or two. He was considered a business success.

The estate at the edge of the sea was in the nature of a hunting preserve. Within its bounds was some of the roughest land in Canada. The shore was a ragged stone wall which shot up out of the water. The coast was fanged with reefs and tiny islands.

The estate itself was a collection of pinnacle and canyons, boulders and brush. Alex Savage boasted freely that there were parts of his estate upon which he had never set eyes. Moreover, he claimed there were spots which no one had ever explored. This was possible, since there were places to which none could climb.

In this labyrinth of stone and brush, Alex Savage had erected a log cabin. In it, he spent part of each summer, and all of the hunting seasons. The cabin had several rooms. It was fitted with electric lights, electric refrigeration, radio, and even air-conditioning apparatus, although there was seldom need for the latter. The rugs were rich. Any one who sat in one of the luxurious chairs was in danger of sinking from sight. The place was no backwoodsman's hut.

From the wide veranda of the cabin, an excellent view could be had of the sea. Monster boulders and tall trees towered around the place; thick underbrush made these surroundings almost a jungle. Twilight came to the brush almost an hour before the sun actually set.

The birds usually made a good deal of noise settling for the night.

It was twilight now, but the birds were making no noise. The feathered songsters had been chilled into silence by an eerie sound.

This noise pealed out erratically. At times, there was five minutes of dead silence. Then weird, unearthly cries would shiver out, a babbling volley of them. They had a human quality, those cries. They were tremulous with an incoherent horror.

The bird life could not have been more silent had death been astalk.

The latest outburst of the banshee cries was somewhat more human than before. They sounded very like some one in frightful agony.

Inside the Alex Savage cabin, a feminine voice called sharply: "Boat Face! Haven't you got that rifle fixed yet?"

There was no answer.

"Boat Face!" the girl called again angrily.

There was a moment of silence. Then a squaw shuffled out of the kitchen region. She was very fat, very brown, and wore enough clothes to garb several of her white-skinned sisters. She looked as competent as the Rock of Gibraltar.

"Boat Face, him in kitchen, Miss Patricia," she said calmly. "Him scared out of skin."

"Boat Face won't go out and investigate those cries?" the girl asked.

"Him heap big coward," said the squaw.

The girl stepped back from a window. She had a wealth of bronze hair—hair very closely akin in hue to that of Doc Savage. She had been watching the brush that circled like a wall.

She was tall; her form was molded along lines that left nothing to be desired. Her features were as perfect as though a magazine-cover artist had designed them.

She wore high-laced boots, breeches, and a serviceable gray shirt.

A cartridge belt was draped about her waist. From it dangled a heavy Frontier Single Action six-shooter—freely admitted by those who know to be one of the most reliable guns ever made. In the crook of her right arm lay a very modern automatic big-game rifle.

"I'll talk to him, Tiny," said the girl.

"O. K., Miss Patricia," said Tiny. "It do no good. That damn half-breed husband of mine plenty afraid."

Tiny was the cook. Boat Face was man-of-all-work around the place. These two were the only servants.

Patricia's heels tapped angrily into the kitchen.

Boat Face was a squarish, copper-colored man, who sat in a corner, holding a rifle. His squaw, Tiny, had called him a breed, but he looked pure Indian. Just what had given him the name of Boat Face was a mystery only an Indian could fathom. His beady black eyes refused sullenly to meet Patricia's gaze.

Patricia started to speak—then held back her words.

The eerie, banshee cries once more babbled from the gloomy brush outside the cabin. They were unmistakably human now, appealing for succor.

Boat Face's ink-black eyes wavered. He took a firmer grasp on a rifle which lay across his knees.

"I no go out," he muttered. "Rifle broke."

Patricia Savage suddenly siezed Boat Face's rifle. She examined the mechanism, threw it to her shoulder, and snapped it.

"You're lying!" she cried. "There's nothing wrong with this gun!"

"He heap big piker," grunted Tiny.

Boat Face's eyes rolled nervously.

"That noise—him werewolf," he mumbled.

"Nonsense!" Patricia said sharply. "There is no such animal!"

Boat Face did not seem convinced. "Your pa—if him alive, him no ask me go and see what make that noise."

The words seemed to wash Patricia's rage away. She paled

visibly. Even the fingers which held the rifle tensed to whiteness.

"These sounds have something to do with the murder of my father!" she said shrilly.

"Me no go outdoors," Boat Face mumbled. "You tie can on me, if you like. Me no go, anyway."

"I won't discharge you," Patricia told him in a weary voice. "After all, I won't ask you to do anything I wouldn't do myself. You can stay here. I'll go out and investigate."

Tiny waddled over to a corner. She came back with a double-barrel shotgun and said stoically: "Me go, too!"

"Thanks, Tiny," Patricia said gratefully. "But you and Boat Face stay here on guard."

Tiny nodded reluctantly. Boat Face looked much relieved.

Patricia moved into the cabin's large living room, and drew the shades carefully. Then she indicated one of the uprights which formed a rustic support for the ceiling. This was a log over a foot thick, still covered with natural bark.

"Guard that, especially," she said meaningly.

Tiny and Boat Face showed no surprise—they seemed to comprehend fully what she meant.

Patricia pocketed several extra ammunition clips for her automatic rifle. Then she opened the door and stepped swiftly outside.

Tiny watched her go with evident concern. Boat Face's aboriginal features were inscrutable.

Sunlight still penetrated to the clearing immediately adjacent to the cabin. Gloom lurked in the tangle of rocks and brush beyond. Walking away from the cabin was like leaving a lantern and going into the night.

Patricia walked warily, rifle alert. She kept fingers on safety and trigger. Her ears strained to catch the next outburst of the unearthly cries.

Off to her right, the noise arose. It was low, sinister; a horrible bleating. It persisted only a moment, then whimpered itself into nothingness.

Patricia shivered. She tripped the rifle safety. This time the cry had not sounded so human. Indeed, it seemed to have taken on a repulsive, animallike quality.

The sound had come from inland. From, perhaps, a hundred yards away—maybe more! The girl could not tell.

She went toward the noise, her pretty face so set it was almost a mask. When she was near the spot from which the sound had seemed to come, she searched for tracks. The terrain was not the sort to show a trail; it was too rocky.

Patricia heard the cries again. They now wailed from a little farther on. She advanced—again she found nothing.

A bit later, the sounds came once more. They had moved on ahead. Patricia shuddered. It seemed the eerie crying thing was trying to decoy her away.

Patricia suddenly gave it up as a bad job. She went back toward the cabin, steps hurried, eyes roving uneasily.

She was baffled, and more than a little terrified, and drew a sigh of relief when the cabin came in sight.

"Tiny! Boat Face!" she called. "It's me!"

She did not want the sullen Boat Face or the competent Tiny taking a shot at her by mistake.

Patricia reached the cabin and shoved the door open. She went in—and jerked to a stop. Her pretty features became blankly startled.

The cabin interior looked as if the proverbial cyclone had hit it.

Patricia's eyes wandered. Then she saw something which caused her to cry out shrilly in horror.

Tiny and Boat Face were brown, unmoving forms on the floor!

Stuffing was ripped from rich chairs. Rugs had been plucked up and flung aside. Drawers had been emptied on the floor. Everywhere signs showed the cabin had been searched wildly.

Patricia ran to the voluminous, copper-hued Tiny, and felt anxiously for pulse.

"They're dead!" she wailed miserably.

Within a moment, however, she realized this was a mistake. There was a heartbeat—very faint.

Getting ice cubes from the electric refrigerator, Patricia Savage rubbed them over the faces of Boat Face and Tiny.

Pulse strengthened slowly under the copper skins.

Confident both servants would recover, Patricia ran through the cabin. Everywhere, there was wild upheaval and destruction. From attic down, the search had missed little. The covered motor of the electric refrigerator was even torn open.

There was no trace of the men—certainly it seemed the work of more than one—who had ransacked the place. They must have come in through the rear door, or an unlocked window.

Something like twenty minutes elapsed before Tiny and Boat Face were revived enough to speak coherently.

"What on earth occurred?" Patricia demanded.

The two servants exchanged blank looks.

"Dunno," Boat Face mumbled. "Me and squaw just go to sleep."

Patricia snapped: "That's ridiculous!"

"Boat Face tell truth," said the ample Tiny, with a roll of jet eyes. "We get heap much sleepy and fall over."

Patricia stared fixedly at the floor near where the two servants had been lying. She had discovered something she had not observed before. The sight of the thing had a striking effect. She stood erect, tense, gripping her rifle.

It was a weird, blackish smudge—more than a foot high and half as wide. The thing had the contour of a wolf's head. The features were grotesquely human.

"It's the werewolf's head again!" Patricia said shrilly. "It's the same mark which we began seeing shortly before my father's death—and which we have seen since!"

Boat Face mumbled. "Werewolf! Indian know them. They devil-man with body of wolf. They prowl in woods and eat plenty hunter and trapper."

"Camp-fire ghost tales!" Patricia snapped. "There are no such creatures! This particular werewolf is very human, Boat Face. You and Tiny both know what he is after."

Patricia went to the large bark-covered timber which supported the living-room ceiling. It was this timber which she had asked Tiny and Boat Face to guard.

It had not been disturbed, although the search had missed little else.

Patricia pressed certain projections on the bark. A concealed door flew open. She withdrew from within what looked like a solid block of ivory. The white cube was perhaps two inches square.

"They're after this," Patricia said grimly.

Chapter 6

SQUARE WHITE DEATH

For once, Tiny's aboriginal face lost its stoic indifference. She stared at the ivory cube as if it were a charm which guaranteed the coming of evil events.

"Him bad medicine," she muttered, indicating the snow-white block.

"I cannot understand what significance it has." Patricia turned the cube slowly in her slender fingers. "It seems solid —there is no hollow sound when it is tapped."

"You know where your dad get him?" Tiny asked.

"Father found it under a ledge about two miles from here, years ago," Patricia replied. "It lay amid a cluster of human skeletons. The skeletons looked as if they had been there for centuries. No one knew anything about them."

"Sure!" said Tiny. "That how he find it. That alone enough make it bring bad luck."

Patricia eyed the white cube thoughtfully.

"Dad never dreamed the thing was of any value," she said. "Three weeks ago, he found a prowler searching this cabin. The fellow escaped. A little later, dad received a mysterious demand for the cube. He refused to turn it over."

"Better if him give it up," muttered Boat Face.

Patricia nodded miserably. "Maybe. We began finding those mysterious werewolf marks around the place. We got other demands for the cube. Then we found dad dead. The doctors called it heart failure."

"They make blood bubble," said Tiny. She nodded elaborately. "Your pa, him murdered."

"I think so, too, Tiny," Patricia said jerkily.

"You bet!" The squaw nodded again. "Him die from same thing that almost get me and Boat Face a minute ago."

"You mean the thing that made you unconscious?"

Again Tiny nodded. "You bet."

"But what was it?" Patricia pondered.

"We go to sleep," said Tiny, as if that explained everything.

Nor did Patricia come any nearer a solution of the mystery, although she asked many questions, and finally went outside and searched the immediate neighborhood.

The rocky earth bore no footprints. That meant nothing, however. The marauders could easily have avoided leaving tracks.

The weird banshee crying had not come from the gloomy brush since Patricia had returned to the cabin. The blush of dusk still spread over the sea.

Unexpectedly, a long, doleful sound moaned out, causing echoes to bang against the cliffs. The noise was greatly different from the earliest banshee cries, yet Patricia started violently.

The sound repeated itself a moment later. She knew, then, what it was.

"The trader's launch!" she exclaimed. "They're letting us know that they have some mail."

So rugged was this region in which the Savage cabin lay, that no automobile could penetrate. A stout wagon could get through, but only with difficulty. To come and go, either a speed boat or a seaplane was the most feasible conveyance. A rustic boathouse on the beach held a fast launch.

Mail was delivered to the Savage hunting lodge in an ingenious fashion. A trader who lived up the coast made regular daily trips to the settlement. His route was past the Savage place.

A few hundred feet from shore, there was a floating buoy box. In this, the trader was accustomed to leave the Savage mail.

The estate had no other communication with the outside world. During his sojourns there, Alex Savage had always made it a point not to be disturbed. The place was his refuge from business worries.

Patricia secured binoculars, and focused them on the trader's boat. There was light enough for her to make it out distinctly.

She saw the trader place at least one piece of mail in the box. Then his boat went on.

"Get the launch!" Patricia commanded Boat Face. "I'm going to keep my eyes on the mail box until we get out to it. That's another mysterious thing that has happened. Our mail has been disappearing!"

Boat Face was slow about complying with the order; he seemed reluctant to leave the cabin. Only when Tiny shouted angrily, "You big bum! You do what Miss Pat say!" did he shuffle off toward the boat.

It was fully five minutes before the breed got the launch out of the boathouse and alongside the little wharf in front of the cabin.

During this time, Patricia had not removed her binoculars from the inspection of the buoy box.

"I'm betting nobody got that mail this time!" she declared.

She kept her glasses fixed on the box as Boat Face guided the launch out. At no time had she seen anything suspicious.

The floating mail box was an ordinary buoy with a container countersunk in the top. It turned and bobbed with the waves, being anchored by a light chain to a heavy concrete weight.

Capturing the box with the aid of a boat hook, Patricia opened it.

The container was empty!

"But this is impossible!" Patricia exclaimed incredulously. "I saw mail put in it. I've watched it since. Every instant!"

"Werewolf!" mumbled Boat Face, and shrugged beefy shoulders.

Patricia examined the buoy box. The mail container had

no lock, since thieves were scarce in this region. However, a wave could not possibly have tossed the mail out.

Patricia had Boat Face run the launch in a big circle. She could not find a thing to shed light on the mystery.

Her face was somewhat white as the launch swerved shoreward.

"I can't understand it," Patricia said grimly.

"Werewolf!" muttered Boat Face. "Him heap bad customer."

The girl ignored the redskin's prognostications. She leveled her binoculars inquiringly at the shore line. The cliffs were cracked here and there by canyons, scratched by watercourses. Huge boulders were piled at the foot of the cliffs. Some of these were fully as large as city apartment houses.

"I don't see a thing," she said.

"Werewolf, him can disappear," said Boat Face.

"You say 'werewolf' to me again, and I'm going to have Tiny work out on you!" snapped Patricia.

Boat Face subsided uneasily. Boat Face was something rare in the brotherhood of red men—a henpecked husband. Most bucks make their squaws walk a chalk line, but not Boat Face. On occasion, the lethargic Tiny would shed her stoical air long enough to give Boat Face what metropolitan cops call a "good shellacking." The implement which Tiny used was the same as that employed by her paleface sisters, a rolling pin.

"Did you ever hear of Doc Savage?" Patricia asked suddenly.

"Me no hear of him," said Boat Face, flinching as if he had felt his squaw's rolling pin.

"He's a cousin of mine," said Patricia. "He lives in the United States. I understand he does remarkable things."

"What kind of things?" asked Boat Face.

"He gets people out of trouble."

"Unh!" Boat Face grunted expressively. "How him make money out of business like that?"

"He doesn't do it for money, if what I've heard is true," Patricia announced. "He goes all over the world and helps others, and doesn't charge them anything. He just does it for the excitement."

"Sound like him crazy," Boat Face offered.

Patricia frowned at the servant.

"You're getting a bit insolent lately, Boat Face!" she said pointedly.

"You t'ink so, eh?" Boat Face asked indifferently.

"I don't think—I know!" the girl snapped.

"Me not care what damn gal t'inks!" said Boat Face, plainly sneering.

Bronze-haired Patricia sprang suddenly to her feet. She shot forward like a metallic tigress. Her small right fist swung with the timing and precision of a trained boxer's.

Boat Face saw it coming. He tried to dodge, was a fraction too late. *Pop!* Patricia's knuckles caught him in the right eye.

The blow had snap and power. Boat Face's arm flailed, he wavered off balance, then toppled overboard.

Patricia ran to the rudder as the launch left the floundering brave behind. She turned the craft back, came alongside, and, with her boat hook, hauled Boat Face over the gunwale.

"You apologize for swearing at me," she gritted, "or I'll knock you overboard again!"

Boat Face squirmed. He was a greatly embarrassed redskin. If this ever got out, the other Indians would laugh him out of Canada. He had not dreamed Miss Patricia was such a hellcat.

"Me sorry!" he muttered.

"Starting right now, you are going to jump quick when I give you an order!" Patricia informed him.

"Yes'm," said Boat Face meekly.

"The first thing you are going to do in the morning is to take the launch down the coast to the nearest telegraph office, and send a telegram," Patricia advised.

"Who telegram go to?"

"To Doc Savage," Patricia said grimly. "I need his help!"

In preparing for the night, the cabin windows and doors were locked. This done, it seemed impossible that any one could enter without creating an alarm. Patricia did not think it necessary for the two servants and herself to stand guard.

Night came, a tidal wave of gloom that poured in from the eastward. Darkness crawled down the canyons like predatory black monsters stalking the sun.

Boat Face had quarters in a small room at the rear of the cabin. His ample mate occupied the same cubicle.

Tiny was a substantial squaw. It was doubtful if anything would ever excite her enough to spoil her sleep. She began to snore with astonishing promptness soon after she had retired.

Boat Face had been careful to remain awake. He knew how soundly his squaw slept. After Tiny had snored a half dozen times, Boat Face eased silently out of his small room and crept to the door of the chamber occupied by Patricia Savage. He listened intently, an ear mashed to the wooden panel.

Regular breathing assured him Patricia was asleep.

Careful to make no noise, Boat Face sidled to the bark-covered pillar in the living room. Fumbling until he located the secret catch, he pressed it. The concealed door in the timber flew soundlessly open.

"Heap good!" Boat Face breathed. "Still here. Me use him for bait to croak um damn werewolf! Yah—Boat Face not as dumb as ever'body seem t'ink around here."

Patricia had replaced the ivory cube.

Boat Face withdrew the white block. He fingered it, hefted it. An evil grin warped his swarthy face. He swiped a greedy tongue over his lips.

He seemed to indulge in deep thought for a time. Then he returned the cube to its hiding place, and closed the cleverly constructed door. After this, he let himself out into the night.

His first stop was at the boathouse. There, he carefully unscrewed the plug in the gasoline storage barrel, and let the fluid gurgle out. Then he emptied the launch tank.

"Nobody go from here to send telegram for Doc Savage," he chuckled. "Not right away soon, anyhow. Now, me go fix trap!"

Quitting the boathouse, he faded into the brush. The night swallowed him.

Boat Face was gone nearly an hour. When he appeared again in the vicinity of the cabin, his manner was equally furtive as before. He felt of his clothing, and made a disgusted face. He was soaked with water to the armpits.

"Trap, him all O. K.," he chuckled. Then he stood in the murk near the cabin, pondering.

"Damn squaw will want to know how me get wet," he muttered once. "Me no tell—she use rolling pin."

As if to banish that possibility, Boat Face started to remove his wet clothing. The process was hardly under way, however, when a low hissing came out of the gloom. It was faint, and had apparently originated some distance away.

Boat Face's manner showed that he had heard this hiss before, and that it had a definite meaning. He fastened the buttons he had loosened, then crept off in the gloom, toward the source of the hiss.

His objective proved to be a clump of spruce two hundred yards distant. These trees narrowly missed growing as thick as hair. Boat Face came to a stop near the dense covert.

"What you want?" he called in a low, grouchy tone.

Out of the sepia of the spruce came harsh words: "Have you found where that ivory cube is hidden?"

Boat Face stood in sullen silence. Apparently he was giving the matter thought.

"Me know!" he said finally.

"For crying out loud!" snarled the man in the thicket. "Why didn't you lemme know! Had you found it before we searched the cabin this evening?"

Boat Face seemed to give this thought, too.

"No!" he lied.

"Well, go bring me the block," the unseen man directed.

"Me get five hundred dollars!" Boat Face reminded.

"O. K.! O. K.!" snarled the other. "Get the ivory cube. I've got your mazuma for you. Five hundred good Canadian dollars."

Boat Face shuffled off.

The wily redskin servant succeeded in entering the cabin without arousing anybody. He went directly to the hiding place in the rustic ceiling support and got the ivory cube. Then, easing outdoors again, carrying the ivory block, he shuffled for the spruce-thicket rendezvous.

Before Boat Face had covered many yards, however, he came to a stop. His tongue traveled greedily over his thick lips. He scratched the end of his hook nose, fingering the white cube.

"Ugh!" he grunted. "Five hundred dollar not enough! Him worth a million. Them guys bad actors. But me got way to fix um."

He nodded profoundly over this bit of logic.

"Me make that feller pay more," he decided.

Boat Face turned at right angles toward the beach. He had never moved more soundlessly. The wilderness of boulders along the edge of the little bay swallowed his slinking form.

There was silence then, except for the calling of a night bird somewhere and the suck of small waves at rock crevices. Several times, there were splashings; these were such as might be made by leaping fish. A breeze shuffled leaves together, making a noise like mice running on paper.

Like a red-skinned ghost, Boat Face materialized in the vicinity of the spruce thicket.

"How!" he called.

"You got the cube?" asked the harsh voice of the unseen man.

"Me got him," Boat Face admitted.

"Cough up, then. I've got the five hundred you were to get for delivering it."

"Five hundred not enough," pronounced Boat Face.

The man in the thicket cursed softly. "So you're a welsher, eh?"

"Welsher—what him?" asked Boat Face.

"It's a guy who makes an agreement and don't go through with it," the other gritted. .

"Me want ten thousand dollars," Boat Face announced.

A choking sound came out of the spruce. "So Jesse James has put on feathers!"

"Me no like funny guys," Boat Face said sullenly. "Ten thousand dollars! Put up or shut up!"

"Now listen, Indian!" the other argued angrily. "We played square with you. We even took you into our confidence and told you what the ivory block is, and why we wanted it. And now you're welshing!"

"Put up or shut up!" Boat Face insisted.

The unseen man was briefly silent.

"Shut up it is!" he said abruptly.

There was a sharp swishing sound—a note that was half a whistle. It was followed by a dull thud which resembled a rock falling into mud.

Boat Face pitched soundlessly backward. The hilt of a knife protruded from his chest over the heart, and he gave only a few weak squirmings while he died.

The killer crawled from the spruce thicket at once. He kept on hands and knees, making him seem sinister, more spiderlike than human. He had a handkerchief bound over his face, mask fashion.

"Shut up, it was!" he snarled at the lifeless Boat Face. "A shut-up for you!"

With eager fingers he searched for the ivory cube. Searched again! He fell to cursing in a low, guttural voice which had suddenly betrayed a trace of foreign accent.

Then he cursed aloud.

The ivory cube was not in Boat Face's clothing.

Some minutes later, a curious conclave took place in a deep canyon far up on the mountain side. The meeting was held on the water-worn stone bottom of the canyon. Stygian realms never produced a more intense darkness than that which gorged the scene of the conference.

Several men were present. Not one of them could see his fellows in the ebony void.

"I made a hell of a bad move!" announced the man who

had thrown the knife that brought death to Boat Face. "I should have searched him before I croaked him."

"You are telling us!" snarled another voice.

"How was I to know he didn't have the ivory cube?" the killer defended.

"The milk is spilled, hombres. Why cry?" said a man with a marked Spanish accent.

"That's an idea!" agreed the slayer. "The redskin probably didn't have the cube at all. My guess is that the girl still has it. We'll soon get it from her!"

"Si, si! But what if the Señorita Savage does not know where it is?"

"She knows. Her old man would tell her."

"Possibly. And it is possible, too, that we made a mistake in disposing of the Señor Alex Savage in such haste."

"He caught me talkin' to that redskin, didn't he?" snarled Boat Face's slayer. "It looked like my best move to put him out of the way and let the redskin get the cube."

"Si, si!" agreed the other amiably. "You are not being criticized, my friend. Our chief may not like this, however. But we will consider other matters. You got the letter from the buoy box?"

The query was addressed to another member of the sinister gathering.

"Sure," replied the man who had been spoken to. "It wasn't a letter, though. It was a telegram."

The man now thumbed on a flashlight. The brilliant beam, splattering at his feet, disclosed a contrivance which vaguely resembled a gas mask. This was a self-contained diving lung.

The diving lung held the explanation of how the man had gotten the letter from the buoy box without being seen by Patricia Savage. He had merely weighted himself, marched to the float underwater, climbed the mooring line, and reached into the box. In the poor light of dusk, Patricia had not seen his hand enter the container.

The man extracted a telegram from a pocket. "This is it."

A gnarled brown hand whipped out and snatched both the telegram and the man's flashlight. The telegram was exposed under the beam.

"Que lastima!" exploded the man who had seized the message. "What a pity! This is from Doc Savage to his uncle, whom he evidently does not know is dead. But it asks if the esteemed uncle got the telegram in which the Señor Doc Savage said he was coming for a visit."

"They did not!" chuckled a man. "We secured that message as we did this one."

"It is evident that Señor Doc Savage suspects something is wrong," said the one who had read the telegram. "That is bad."

Someone laughed fiercely.

"The boss will take care of that!"

"*Si, si!*" agreed the man with the telegram. "He is very ingenious, that maestro of ours. He will thoroughly dispose of this Doc Savage."

A few minutes later, the sinister gathering dispersed.

Chapter 7

STRANGE ATTACKERS

The train was still driving its way westward, excitement and tragedy hovering over it.

Girl-faced El Rabanos waved his arms and screamed: "This man Savage is the murderer!"

Renny shook fists that were larger than brickbats, rumbling: "Say that again, sissy-faced squirt, and I'll hit you so hard you'll turn into a grease spot!"

Monk's pig, Habeas Corpus, squealed violently.

Señor Corto Oveja glared and shrilled: "I, too, think Señor Savage is the murderer."

Pretty Señorita Oveja put hands over her mouth to crowd back sobs. She made no accusations either way.

The train was in a general uproar—it had been thus for more than two hours.

The dead form of Wilkie, the conductor, was still sprawled in its crimson puddle on the Pullman washroom floor. His murderer was as yet uncaught.

With the noisy violence of Latin temperaments, Señor Oveja and El Rabanos had shouted the length of the train that Doc Savage was the killer. They were still shouting insistently. The very noisiness of their assertion was producing an effect.

"This man Savage suggested the mission on which the conductor was killed!" El Rabanos repeated for probably the dozenth time.

"That mission was ridiculous in the first place!" snapped Señor Oveja. "It was to summon and question all Spanish people on this train."

"I notice there's a lot of them," Renny said pointedly.

"You have heard their story!" El Rabanos snapped. "They are going to a convention of a Spanish society being held on the Pacific coast."

This was true. On the train were about a dozen individuals of Spanish ancestry. Without exception, they declared they were going to the meeting of the society. The news butcher on the train had found a story in one of his papers which proved there actually was such a meeting scheduled.

Doc was not under arrest. But that was simply because there happened to be no officers on the train.

The most unpleasant of recent developments, from Doc's standpoint, was the work of Señor Oveja. The señor had dispatched a telegram to the Mounted Police at the train's next stop, asking that officers be on hand to arrest Doc. This was a through train. It had not paused since the discovery of Wilkie's body. Señor Oveja had dropped his message at a small depot as the train had flashed past it.

Renny sidled close to Doc.

"This is beginning to look bad!" he said in a low voice. "There is not the slightest clue to show who murdered Wilkie."

Girl-faced El Rabanos sprang forward, shouting: "These men should not be allowed to talk together! They may plot an escape!"

Doc Savage shrugged wearily and sat down.

"Would you mind bringing a glass of water, Renny?" he asked.

"Glad to!" said Renny.

There was a long glass cylinder mounted in a corner of the coach. This held paper cups which dropped out when one inserted a penny. Renny ignored these. He wandered off to the regions of the diner.

After a bit, Renny was back, carrying a plain glass beaker, brimful of cold water.

Doc drank the water. Holding the empty glass in both hands, he toyed with it as he addressed entrancingly pretty Señorita Oveja.

"I wonder if you would do me a favor?" he asked.

"What?" the young woman inquired shortly.

"Tell me why you think I am your enemy."

El Rabanos put in wrathfully: "That is information which we shall give to the Mounted Police!"

"Would I like to smear that face of yours!" Renny thundered at El Rabanos.

"Here," Doc said, and handed Renny the glass.

Renny took the beaker. There was a strange expression on his long, puritanical face.

Renny departed as if he were returning the water glass to where he had gotten it.

Seemingly with no particular purpose in mind, gaunt Johnny and pale Long Tom sauntered off together.

Twirling his sword cane, Ham was next to leave the group. The pig Habeas Corpus under an arm, Monk trailed after the dapper lawyer. Ham was inviting Monk to quit following him around as they passed out of hearing.

"We should keep an eye on those men!" El Rabanos declared.

"Fat chance they've got of getting off the train!" somebody told him. "We're hitting all of sixty miles an hour."

Doc Savage went to a writing desk and selected a book of telegram blanks. He addressed a message to the Mounted Police at the metropolis where the train next stopped.

ADVISE YOU HAVE STATION AND VICINITY BRILLIANTLY LIGHTED WHEN OUR TRAIN ARRIVES STOP ALSO HAVE ENOUGH TROOPERS ON HAND TO SEE THAT NO ONE ESCAPES STOP CONFIDENT SOMETHING CRIMINAL UNDERFOOT

DOC SAVAGE

Doc tied the telegram in his handkerchief, first weighting it with two silver dollars. Then he opened the window. He did this in plain view, not wishing to have somebody get excited and take a shot at him. He consulted his watch, then waited. He had studied the timetable earlier, and knew they were due to pass through a small town in a few moments.

The train whistle moaned. A pinpoint eye of light opened in the distance. This approached with a rush. It was the illuminated window of a railway station. The little depot looked like a match box in the headlight glare.

Standing in front of the station was a man who wore a green eyeshade, and had black dust protectors over his shirt sleeves. The accoutrements stamped him as the telegraph operator.

Doc threw his message as the train hooted past. Considering the terrific speed, his aim was uncanny. The handkerchief, the telegram inside, all but bounced into the operator's hands.

In the act of closing the window, Doc noted something from the corner of an eye.

Señor Oveja was bending over the desk where the telegram had been written. He hastily sauntered away from the desk when he saw Doc observing him.

Doc gave no sign of having noticed. He knew what Señor Oveja was doing at the desk. There had been a sheet of carbon paper in the pad upon which Doc had written his message. Señor Oveja had read this carbon copy of Doc's wire.

It was possible the señor imagined he had done a neat bit of detecting. As a matter of fact, Doc had left the carbon copy deliberately uncovered, and had been careful that the señor saw it. Doc wanted to see what Señor Oveja's reaction would be. He learned little. The señor kept his thoughts well concealed.

Throughout the next half hour, Doc Savage remained within sight of the writing desk. He wanted to observe any others who might seek to get a look at the carbon copy.

No one else went near the desk.

The train charged recklessly through the night, swooping across bridges with a thunderous moan, and panting noisily over grades.

Some sage once wrote that the presence of death makes people silent. He should have been on that train. He would have heard more conversation than at a chamber-of-commerce luncheon. In smokers, diners, Pullmans, day coaches, discussion waged. A number of uninformed persons had never heard of Doc Savage. These were speedily enlightened by their neighbors.

One man spoke steadily for five minutes, reciting the remarkable ability of Doc Savage, and the things he had accomplished. He finished with: "This man Savage is a person of mystery. Not much is known about him."

"Oh, yeah!" snorted his listener. "A mystery, eh? And you just told me more about him than you can tell me about the Prince of Wales."

"What I mean is—Savage don't parade his feats around in public," the other explained. "He don't brag. For instance, take his five helpers. There's an engineer, a chemist, a lawyer, a geologist, and an electrical expert. What do you know about them?"

"I have heard this: in their respective lines, they are among the most learned men in the world," was the reply.

"That's right," declared the first man. "Yet Doc Savage is a greater expert in these lines—engineering, chemistry, law, archæology, and electricity—than his aides, and he's just as proficient in many other lines. They say he is, beyond a doubt in the least, the greatest living surgeon."

"Sounds like a fairy tale."

"Sure it does!" agreed the other. "Just the same, I don't

think this bronze man murdered the conductor, and I'd hate to be the fellow who did. Savage will get him, sure."

Heedless of this discussion, and many others along similar lines, Doc Savage returned to his drawing-room. Hardly had he entered when his sharp eyes noted something amiss. A folded newspaper reposed in the wastebasket. He had not placed it there.

His movements unhurried, the bronze man locked the drawing-room door. Then he went to the basket and investigated.

The newspaper was one published in the large town they had passed through some hours before—the division point where unfortunate Wilkie had gone on duty. It was at this town that Señor and Señorita Oveja and El Rabanos had boarded the train.

The newspaper was folded so as to enwrap a knife. The long blade of this was still smeared with gore.

Doc's practiced eye measured the width of the blade. He decided it would exactly fit the wound which had caused Wilkie's death.

Opening one of his many hand bags stacked in the compartment, Doc drew out a powerful magnifying glass. He used it on the knife hilt. Finger prints had been wiped off.

Doc opened the window and threw the knife out into the night, far from the plunging train.

Glancing at his watch, Doc saw they would soon reach the next stop—within thirteen minutes, to be exact.

Precisely nine minutes later, the holocaust broke.

From beneath the train came a sudden scream of steel on steel! It was like the wail of a demented monster. The cars rocked in sickening fashion!

Doc Savage plunged the length of the drawing-room, but brought up lightly against the bulkhead.

In the coaches, passengers were hurled against seats. Parcels and suitcases fell off the overhead racks. In the diners, dishes hit the floors as if tossed by invisible scoop shovels. In the mail cars, clerks brought up in tangles with their sacks.

Doc Savage unlocked the drawing-room door, wrenched it open, and whipped out. The steely screeching underfoot died slowly; the train was coming to an unbelievably quick stop.

Doc leaned from a window. With a final squeal of brakes, the train became entirely stationary.

It was no mean feat of agility which Doc performed now. He managed to stand erect outside on the narrow ledge of the train window. One of his hands stretched up, groped, and found a projection on the roof. The practiced swing of a gymnast put him atop the coach.

From this vantage point he could see, as far as darkness permitted, what was occurring. Somewhat more than a quarter of a mile ahead of the rest of the train, the locomotive was just coming to a standstill. In some manner the engine had become detached. No doubt the air brakes were adjusted to stop the coaches instantly in such an emergency.

Doc Savage ran forward along coach tops. It was his guess that some one, possibly traveling over the tops of the coaches as he was doing, had severed the connection between the engine and cars. Doc hoped to glimpse the malefactor.

At the forward end of the train, Doc dropped to the side of the tracks and conducted a brief examination. There was a film of grease and dust on the connecting mechanism. This was smudged where a hand had grasped it.

From his pocket, Doc produced a small flashlight. It gave an intense white beam, no thicker than a pencil. Whoever had caused the locomotive to separate from the train, had worn gloves. There were no finger prints.

The engine was backing slowly to rejoin its lost string of coaches.

With an ease that would have amazed an onlooker, Doc regained the top of the train. He ran rearward. He was taking no chances. It seemed he had violent enemies on the train. They might chance a shot at him.

Swinging down, he reëntered his drawing-room. No one was there. Plucking a hand bag out of his luggage heap, Doc opened it.

He lifted out a metal contraption which resembled a pocket-size magic lantern. The lens of this was almost black. Doc turned a switch on the side of the contraption. Apparently, nothing happened.

Then Doc went to a shelf over the washbowl and picked up a large water glass. The glass had not been on the shelf when he departed. It was the same beaker in which Renny had brought Doc the drink of water.

Doc held the glass in front of the lens of the thing that looked like a magic lantern. What happened was startling.

To the naked eye there was nothing unusual about the glass. Certainly no writing was visible. But the instant Doc held the beaker before the magic lantern, written letters sprang out in a dazzling, electric blue. The writing at the top was in a script so perfect that it might have been done by an engraver. It was Doc's own handwriting. It read:

All five of you shadow Señor Oveja, his daughter and El Rabanos.

Below this was another communication, done in a more scrawling hand. This one read:

The three of them prepared to leave the train just before it stopped, Doc. It looks suspicious, although they might have intended to get off at the next station. Señor Oveja is wearing a big white panama hat that you can't mistake. We're trailing them.

There was no more. Doc dropped the glass and crushed it to fragments under a heel. Then he switched off the lantern contrivance, pocketed it, and stepped out in the corridor.

Moving swiftly, he began a search of the train.

Doc Savage did many things which to the layman were puzzling and sometimes inexplicable. Always he had a reason for what he did. His method of communicating with his friends by leaving writing on glass—writing quite invisible to the naked eye—was something to amaze one unfamiliar with the bronze giant.

When Doc had asked for water, the big-fisted Renny had understood that what his bronze chief wanted was a tablet on which to write some orders.

The writing was done with a bit of strange chalk. Its markings were almost undetectable—until exposed to ultraviolet light. Then it would fluoresce, showing in blue. The lantern contrivance Doc had used was an ultraviolet projector.

Passengers stood in aisles in the coaches, feeling tenderly of spots which had been bruised when the train stopped so suddenly. A few had clambered out and stood beside the track. Not many had done this. There is something which makes the average man reluctant to leave his train when it stops, a subtle fear that he will get left behind when the train starts again.

Doc Savage walked all the way to the baggage cars, and back again to the observation coach. His giant stature, the remarkable bronze hue of his skin, drew much attention. Passengers stared. Without exception, they had heard the gossip concerning this giant man with the golden eyes.

Everyone knew the bronze man had been accused of stabbing Wilkie to death. But no one showed an inclination to stop Doc. The metallic giant did not look like a safe fellow to meddle with.

Doc reflected that events must have occurred swiftly while he was forward making his unsuccessful hunt for whoever had separated the engine from the train.

Nowhere on the train could be seen Señor Corto Oveja, his attractive daughter, or the girl-faced El Rabanos. They had vanished.

From the group of swarthy passengers who claimed they were en route to the meeting of a Spanish society, four were missing.

Doc's five men were also not to be found. Even the pig, Habeas Corpus, was gone.

Doc came out on the observation platform at the conclusion of his search. He noted a man with a red lantern standing some distance down the track. That would be a flagman sent back to guard against a rear-end collision.

From forward came a low crash. This traveled the length of the train, like a rock bouncing downstairs. The locomotive had hooked on. The whistle blared. The man with the lantern came running back. The train was preparing to go on.

Doc Savage vaulted over the observation platform rail, landing lightly on cinders and gravel. The brakeman, running with his head down, did not see Doc Savage. The passengers who had stepped off the train were too busy climbing back on to notice the departure of the bronze man.

The locomotive whistled again, then began to chug mightily and spew steam. The train moved, slowly at first, but gathering speed. The tail lights went past. They looked like little eyes on a monster snake which was crawling backwards. The serpent monster lost itself and its roaring in the distance.

The blacker gloom in the lee of a large rock seemed to detach itself and scud along the track. Doc Savage had become a soundless phantom. From a coat pocket, he drew the rather bulky black metal box which was his ultraviolet lantern. He switched this on and played its invisible beam before him.

Shortly a tiny, arrow-shaped mark sprang out in dazzling, electric blue. It was drawn on top of a rock with the chalk which Doc and his men employed to exchange secret communications.

Doc glided in the direction which the arrow indicated. Two rods, and he found a second pointer.

From a pocket, Doc extracted his small flashlight. His men —trailing their enemies, no doubt—had left these arrows to indicate the direction they had taken. Doc intended to inspect the track, and find just how many individuals his friends were following. He thumbed the flash on.

To his left a machine gun opened up! Its deadly cackle was like the sound of a gigantic cricket!

Doc Savage seemed to melt down before the hideous gabble of noise and the moaning stream of jacketed lead.

Chapter 8

THE MAN IN THE WHITE HAT

The stuttering of the rapid-firer ended as abruptly as it had started. The last few empty cartridges to jump from the ejector mechanism tinkled brassily on the rocks. There was no sound after that, but the mad flight of a rabbit which had been frightened out of its wits by the sudden uproar. Eventually, that noise also died away.

"Bueno!" hissed a voice. "That, amigos, settles our troubles!"

"Si, si!" a low whisper agreed.

Men advanced. From the sound of their movements, there were four of them. They strode warily.

"Un fosforo!" commanded one. "A match!"

There was a tiny clatter of safety matches in a box. The box scraped open. But no match was lighted.

One of the marauders screeched! The sound was awful—as if invisible hands had seized his heart and were tearing it out. The ghastly peal trailed off in a sob—a sob like water pouring through a pipe.

The other three skulkers were brave enough. They leaped to assist their companion.

"Que hay?" yelled one. "What is the matter?"

He found out soon enough. Something seized his left arm—something which crushed flesh against bone with an awful pressure. The arm went numb with pain. It had no more feeling than a thick cord attached to his body. And by that cord the man was abruptly lifted and flung far to one side.

As he slammed down in brush and rocks, the man was quite sure that it could not have been a human hand which had seized him. It must have been some hulking colossus of the night.

He was wrong.

The other two men became aware of the truth, for their groping hands and striking fists encountered a form unmistakably human.

"En verdad!" choked one. "Indeed! It is the bronze hombre! Our lead missed him!"

The four men, seeing Doc sink as their shots roared, naturally supposed he was done for. Not knowing the blinding speed with which the bronze giant moved, they had been too optimistic.

Doc had been warned in advance by a faint click as a machine-gun safety was released, and had dropped in time to get clear. But some rapid-firer slugs had come so close that his ears still rang with their whine.

One of the would-be killers tried to use his machine gun. The weapon muttered deafeningly! The bullets dug up a cloud of dust.

Doc seized the gun, pulled, and got its hideous gobbling stilled before it could do any damage.

Then came a new development. Somewhere near by, running feet sounded. Reënforcements arriving!

Doc listened, wondering if they were his own men.

They were not. A guttural ejaculation in Spanish told him that.

Flashlight beams—blinding funnels of white—jumped from the hands of the newcomers. The glare illuminated Doc.

One of the new arrivals fired a revolver. Had Doc not pitched violently to one side, that bullet would have ended his career. It was well aimed.

Doc Savage had, for much of his life, walked in the shadow of peril and sudden death. Many men had sought to end his existence by violent means. To kill in defense of his own life, frequently seemed imperative. Yet Doc never did that.

The bronze man's enemies by no means went unscathed. They frequently perished—but always in traps of their own setting. Doc did not take life with his own hands.

Doc still held the machine gun which he had seized. He could have fired upon the approaching gunmen. His chances of downing them were excellent, for there seemed to be only two. But because of the darkness, he knew he would have to kill rather than merely wound.

Flinging aside in a leap that was of almost incredible length, Doc temporarily evaded the white funnels of the flashlights. Doubling low, he raced from the vicinity.

The surrounding terrain was level. Boulders and brush were both small, and would conceal a man only if he lay prone and perfectly still. Doc was forced to race fifty yards before he found adequate cover.

Twice, in that distance, flashlights found him and guns cackled noisily. One bullet cut his coat across the shoulders, but did not open his bronze skin. This was excellent shooting, since Doc was traveling at great speed.

He ducked into the shelter of a boulder, and waited.

The newcomers smashed out more random bullets. They made no effort at pursuit; instead, they helped the four they had rescued to stand erect.

The whole party retreated at a wild run.

Doc promptly set out after them. He deemed it wise to go slowly, for they blasted frequent bullets in his direction. At first, because it would be very dangerous, he made no effort to overhaul the group. Once they reached rough going, he intended to whip close to them.

He suddenly quickened his pace. The rusty squeak of barbed wire against staples had told him the men were mounting a fence.

An automobile engine burst into noisy life! Headlights came on. The car rocketed away.

There was a road beyond the fence, very dusty, but wide and well graded. Doc stood in it and watched the receding car. The tail-light bulb had been extinguished, so he could not read the license number.

A flight of bullets came up the road from the receding auto, and Doc hastily quitted the thoroughfare.

Going back to the scene of the fight, he dabbed his flashlight beam about. Tracks were numerous. Doc's practiced eye measured these for possible future reference. He gathered up several empty machine-gun and revolver cartridges.

Beside a studded bush, he found his chief clew. This was an extremely white Panama hat, wide of brim and high of crown. Inside the sweatband of the hat, printed in gold lettering, was a name:

OVEJA

Thanks to the darkness, Doc had not glimpsed the features of any of his attackers. The first four had been sprawled on the ground when the two rescuers appeared with their flashlights. Had they been on their feet, Doc might have glimpsed their faces.

Doc recalled the message in invisible chalk which one of his five men had left on the water glass. It had stated that Señor Oveja had donned a large white Panama. And who had read Doc's wire asking the Mounted Police to surround the train on arrival? Oveja, of course.

Switching on his ultra-violet lantern, Doc resumed what he had been doing when the attack came—following the arrow markers left by his men. The indicators jumped out in unearthly blue flame at frequent intervals. The route angled away from the railroad tracks and mounted a hill.

Beyond the hill, lights were arrayed like white-hot beads strung on taut wires.

The spots of iridescence were street lamps of the town which the train had been nearing when it had stopped so suddenly. It was not a large metropolis—only a few thousand in population.

Doc Savage followed the luminous arrows down the slope. They turned, paralleling the railroad. When the trail dropped into a small gulley, he used his flashlight, which gave a light as bright as burning magnesium.

The sandy gulch floor was pocked with tracks. To an individual of average perception, they would have looked pretty much alike. An experienced tracker might have known, from the depth of the prints, that two of the men making the tracks were very heavy, and that one was a woman.

Doc Savage, however, read the prints like a chart. He picked out the tracks of his five men—he knew their every peculiarity, from the fact that Monk and Renny, the giants, made deep, big prints, to the straight, military preciseness of Ham's walk, with the little irregularity when the lawyer twiddled his sword cane.

When he had the five segregated, three sets remained. These had been walked over by Doc's aides, so he knew his friends were trailing the three persons. Two of the quarry were men, the other a woman. Her prints were high-heeled and very feminine.

Near the edge of town, the trail turned abruptly and began to circle the settlement.

Doc studied the town, judging its size from the street lights. In small villages, telegrams were usually handled from the railway station. This borough looked large enough to have an office uptown.

Deserting the trail, Doc entered a street and ran along it. His pace would have taxed a proficient sprinter, but, even after he had traversed several blocks, the bronze man's breathing had not quickened appreciably. His mighty muscles were conditioned by regular exercise until they seemed to show no more fatigue than the metal of a machine.

The telegraph office was nested in the front of a brick hotel. It was brilliantly lighted, and relays were cheeping on the instrument table.

On duty was an exceedingly tall and freckled young man, whose hair stood up like the coiffure of a Fiji Islander.

"I want information about certain telegrams which may have come here tonight," Doc told him.

"That is against the rules!" the young man replied promptly.

Doc brought a wallet out. This held numerous cards. He selected one particular pasteboard from the collection in that wallet.

"Does this make it any different?" he asked, and exhibited the card.

The young man looked, then whistled softly. "I'll say it does!"

The card was signed by the highest official of the company, and informed all employees that Doc Savage was to receive every assistance possible, no matter of what nature, or what the possible consequences.

Going behind the counter, Doc sorted through carbon copies of messages received that evening. He found his own communication, addressed to the local Mounted Police. There was also a wire signed by Señor Corto Oveja, asking the Mounties to arrest Doc as soon as the train arrived.

The prize, however, was one signed simply, "John Smith." It was addressed to "Sam Smith." Doc eyed the body of the message. At first glance the thing seemed unintelligible. The stuff sounded like bad poetry.

THE HORSE OF IRON HE SAW THE CITY FLEAS AWAY DID RUN AND THAT VERY SWIFTLY STOP MAN OH MAN WAS THE GAS BUGGY HANDY

Doc read the doggerel again. Its meaning became clear. It was simply a message from John Smith to Sam Smith, advising that the train would be deserted at the edge of town, and that an automobile should be on hand. The Smith names were probably fakes.

"Remember the fellow who recieved this?" Doc asked.

"Yep!" said the operator eagerly. "There was two of them. They came in and asked if there was a message for Sam Smith. I remembered them because of the funny way that message sounded."

"Describe them," Doc requested.

"Both were short and dark-skinned. They wore greasy coveralls. I saw an aviator's helmet sticking from the hip pocket of each man."

"Fliers! And strangers in town, eh?"

"Yes, sir!" The telegrapher was beginning to look awed. "Gee whiz! Say, I just happened to think that I've heard of you. Aren't you the Doc Savage the newspapers carry stories about—the fellow they call the 'Man of Mystery?' Aren't you the man who just got back from Arabia, where you took a submarine and followed an underground river under the desert? And at the end of the river you found——"

"I'll use your wires," Doc told the frizzle-haired operator. He had not changed expression, but he was a bit embarrassed. Hero worship got Doc's goat—when he was the subject of admiration.

He examined the "John Smith" telegram. It had been sent from a small way station on the railroad some fifty miles back.

Doc opened the telegraph key. A moment later, he was in communication with the station from which the message had been sent. He described the missive in which he was interested.

"It was thrown off the fast train," reported the distant telegrapher. "But I didn't get a look at the party who threw it."

"Was it handwritten?" Doc queried over the wire.

"It was printed," the other replied.

Doc closed the key and stood up. Since the message was printed, there was no chance of tracing the author by his handwriting.

The freckled, frizzle-haired young man stared at Doc in open-mouthed amazement. He had been listening to the wire talk. He had just heard some of the fastest and most perfect hand-sent Morse to which he had ever listened. It had been as rapid as if sent with a fast automatic key, a "bug." The freckled young man had not believed such a thing possible.

Leaving the telegraph office and its stunned manager, Doc resumed the luminous-arrow trail left by his friends. He had sprinted the entire distance from the telegraph office. He continued running as he followed the trail.

Around the fringe of the settlement, his course led.

A prowling dog, sighting the bronze man, began to growl fiercely.

"Cut it out, old fellow," Doc called.

The calm friendliness of the mighty man's tone had a marked effect upon the dog. It exchanged tail-wagging for growling. Doc was forced to toss a rock near the dog to keep the suddenly friendly animal from following him. This was another example of the remarkable things his great voice could do.

Unexpectedly, Doc came upon Monk. The homely chemist was sprawled flat on the ground. The pig, Habeas Corpus, lay comfortably beside him.

"Hands up!" Monk growled. "Grab a cloud!" He had failed to recognize Doc.

"Bite him, pig!" Doc ordered dryly.

Habeas Corpus promptly stood up and bit furiously at Monk. Monk dodged. Much to the homely chemist's disgust, somebody had recently taught his pet pig the trick of biting the nearest human when told to do so. Monk was usually the victim of these nips. He suspected the dapper Ham had taught the pig the trick.

"Where is the rest of the gang?" asked Doc.

Monk waved a furry arm in the gloom. "They're watching that joint over there."

Doc peered into the night. He made out a building which resembled a gigantic, square hatbox. "An airplane hangar!"

"Sure," said Monk. "There's a little flying field over there. Señor Oveja, the girl, and El Rabanos are in the hangar."

"You're sure Señor Oveja is there?" Doc asked quickly.

"You bet! We've been right on their heels since they left the train. He couldn't have slipped away."

"Señor Oveja has been wearing his white Panama hat?" Doc queried.

Monk's voice was very small in the murk. "He tossed that aside before he left the train."

"What made him do it?"

"Don't know for sure," Monk said. "It looked like El Rabanos pointed out that the white hat would show up plain in the dark."

Doc informed Monk of the attack which had come as he followed the trail.

"The first four men to jump me might have been off the train," he declared. "From what I learned at the telegraph office, the other two were obviously fliers, waiting near by in a car."

Monk grunted softly. "Renny said he saw a black monoplane that seemed to be following our train. That was just before dark."

"It might have been carrying the two who got the telegram at this town," Doc admitted.

"This thing is sure a mess," Monk muttered. "It shapes up like this: Señor Oveja, his daughter, and El Rabanos are after you. Another gang is after them, and also you."

"And the motivation behind the whole thing is a deep,

black mystery," Doc agreed. "Let's collar the three in the hangar, here, and see what we can dig out of them."

As if touched off by the decision, a hollow roaring burst from the airplane hangar.

"Blazes!" Monk barked. "They've started up a plane!" He raced for the hangar.

The pig, Habeas Corpus, bounced after him, squealing and grunting with each jump.

Doc joined Monk in the race. Both heard metal doors on the hangar rasp open. A plane jumped out of the structure. Its exhaust stack was a fiery mouth that slavered sparks! Its roar was like cannonading!

Except for one thing, Doc and his men might have seized the plane's occupants. It was doubtful if those in the craft knew of the presence of their pursuers. Had the wind been coming from straight ahead, they would undoubtedly have stopped in front of the hangar to warm the engine, before taking off. But the wind was in the opposite direction; it was necessary to taxi across the field before taking the air. The pilot decided to warm his engine while doing that.

Away the ship went. It rolled too swiftly even for Doc's fleet running. Landing lights jutted fans of incandescence from the wing tips of the airplane.

Reaching the far edge of the tarmac, the plane taxied around and took off. It was a large yellow biplane, with a cabin for six.

Chapter 9

THE IVORY-CUBE TRAIL

Doc Savage's other men came pounding through the night. Big-fisted Renny was leading.

"Five of us!" Renny boomed disgustedly. "And we let 'em get away!"

"Six of us!" Doc corrected.

"We could have shot 'em down, of course," rumbled Renny. "But the girl was aboard the plane."

The sky was like an overturned bowl of black cotton. Into it, the moaning yellow biplane crawled.

"Let's see if there's another plane in the hangar," Doc rapped.

They raced back for the black box of a hangar. Reaching it, Doc cast his flash beam into the structure.

"There's a crate!" Renny thundered. "No! Two of 'em!"

The planes were small. One was a monoplane, the other an open cockpit. Neither accommodated more than two passengers.

Renny ran to the biplane. It looked the speedier. He latched out the choke, then bounded around in front to spin the prop. But his huge hands only dropped listlessly from the metal blade. He glared at the engine itself.

"Holy cow!" he muttered. "They've got us stumped!"

Doc came around and inspected the plane engine.

"They did it very simply, too," he said dryly. "They just smashed all the spark plugs. There's no need of replacing them. The other plane will be gone before we can get in the air."

Doc had been moving as he spoke. His last word came from near the door.

The other five hastily followed. The bronze man's rapid movements showed he had a plan.

"What's up?" Monk demanded.

"Let's see how fast you are on those bow legs of yours!" Doc suggested.

Heading for town, Doc set a pace which he judged was about the fastest speed the others could travel. It was not slow; they were all adept at running.

Monk, short gorilla legs going like pistons, brought up the rear. At his heels trailed Habeas Corpus. The pig could run like a dog. But, as before, the porker was squealing with every jump.

"Cut that out, or I'll kick you loose from your appetite!" Monk advised the homely shoat.

Habeas Corpus at once stopped squealing.

"That pig has brains, I'm telling you!" Monk shouted.

"That's more than can be said for the guy who owns him!" Ham replied nastily.

The purpose of their pell-mell progress was still a mystery to Doc's five men. They exchanged puzzled looks when Doc entered town and went straight to the telegraph office.

"Do you know the surrounding country?" Doc asked the frizzle-haired operator.

The young man replied: "I've hunted over most of it."

"Mountainous and timbered, isn't it?"

"You bet!"

"I want you to point out all fields which are level enough to land an airplane on," Doc told him. "Don't count the local airport, unless there's more than one."

The young man seized a pencil which dangled from the

counter by a chain, planked a telegraph blank on the counter, and drew a map. His movements were rapid.

"There's only three level places near town," he explained. "One is about a mile north. The other two are at least five miles out. There's only one local airport. You said not to count it, so I'm not."

Doc Savage nodded at Monk and Ham. "You two pals go to the field farthest out. The other three of you take the next one. I'll go to the nearest."

"We're after that black monoplane!" Renny rumbled, suddenly enlightened.

"Right!" Doc agreed. "Grab taxicabs for the trips!"

Doc and his men separated in front of the telegraph office. All but Doc went hunting taxicabs.

Deciding not to bother himself with a cab, Doc headed northward through town. The distance to the field was only a mile. Chances were that he would lose time hunting a hack.

The little metropolis was quiet. Every other street light had been extinguished to conserve electricity. Very few houses were illuminated.

Overhead, the clouds abruptly parted and let moonlight spill down. After the earlier darkness, the moon rays seemed as brilliant as sunlight. Trees along the thoroughfare were scrawny, probably because of the cold winters here in Canada. The shrubs and the houses cast moon shadows.

Dwellings became scattered, then abruptly ceased. Doc crossed a washboard of small black hills. Gullies gaped here and there, as if the skin of the earth had cracked. The road was narrow, graded only in spots. Bridges were crude spans of logs, earth-covered. Apparently the road saw little travel.

Indeed, according to the telegrapher's map, the road terminated shortly beyond the field which was Doc's destination. It was a lane leading to a ranch home.

Doc kept on it, his long strides eating up distance. Soon the road dipped. Two hundred yards ahead in the moonlight, Doc distinguished a gate; beyond that was a patch of level meadow.

A black raven of a monoplane stood at the meadow's edge, some distance from the gate.

Without slackening his pace, Doc came up on his toes, making less noise, thus. He could see no one in or near the black plane, but he was taking no chances.

Small hills reared beyond the meadows. Suddenly the tops of these became weirdly white. It was as if an invisible hand had spilled thin snow upon them.

Then Doc discarded all caution, put on more speed. For he knew what the whiteness meant. A car was coming up the road behind him, and its headlights had bleached the hill.

He heard the engine mumble. The machine was coming fast. Doc had hoped to reach the ebony monoplane; but that, he saw now, was impossible.

The neighborhood was unpleasantly bare of vegetation which might furnish shelter. A mowing machine stood near the gate. Its moon shadow made a spidery hump of gloom. Doc took shelter behind the mowing machine.

The automobile clattered up. Tire treads squealing and throwing dust, it stopped at the gate. The car was a sedan, very shiny with good care, but a model some three years old. It had all the marks of a car hired from a rental agency.

The sedan was jammed with men. In the glare of the moonlight Doc could count six men. All were swarthy-complexioned.

Four of them had been on the passenger train. The other two, attired in greasy coveralls, were obviously the aviators who had called at the telegraph office.

A man clambered from the rear of the car and walked ahead to open the gate.

Doc Savage usually wore a vest of pliable leather under his outer clothing. This vest had numerous pockets, and these held ingenious devices—apparatus with which Doc Savage could cope with almost any emergency. The vest now reposed in his baggage, wherever that might now be. Doc was headed for a vacation, and had not been wearing the vest. He was empty-handed.

There was no doubt but that these six men were armed. Under such conditions, the course of safety was to remain under cover.

Doc quitted the shelter of the mowing machine, and glided up to the car. He had little expectation of reaching the sedan unobserved. Nor did he.

"*Ver!*" cried one of the gang. "See! The bronze devil!"

The men in the machine seemed to go through a convulsion as they grabbed for weapons. The driver let the clutch out; the car went forward like a thing kicked.

Doc had anticipated that the sedan would spring into motion. He had reasoned that by the time it reached the gate, it would be going too swiftly for the man there to spring aboard.

His logic was right—and wrong. The man at the gate was caught off guard. Moreover, he must have been a nervous individual. As the uproar burst forth, he gave one long leap

—in the wrong direction! He was directly in the path of the car!

The sedan hit him, and bore him down as if he were a weed. For a moment after he disappeared, ugly crunchings and crackings came from under the machine. The sounds were those of monster jaws munching. When the unlucky man appeared again—behind the rear bumper—he was shapeless.

Inside the car, guns began a hollow coughing. The windows were up; holes appeared in them. The car pushed its radiator snout through the gate with a roar of splintering wood!

Ducking and weaving, Doc Savage ran after the machine until he reached the gate. The post on which the gate was swung was large, and offered more adequate shelter against bullets than the mowing machine. Doc ducked behind it and made himself as thin as possible.

The car was headed for the plane. It traveled too swiftly for those in it to do accurate shooting. Probably twenty shots were fired. Only two of them hit Doc's post. The rest made short, sharp sounds which were strangely remindful of shrilly barking prairie dogs.

In the road, the man who had been run over was moaning and groaning feebly.

The sedan careened to a stop near the black plane. Using revolvers, four of the men fired steadily in Doc's direction. The other two worked at getting the plane motor started.

Taking a chance, Doc dashed to the man who had been run over. The fellow had carried a revolver—he must have had it in his hand when the car hit him, for the weapon was buried in the dust near by. One of the tires had passed squarely over it.

Doc sought to pick the gun up. But the cylinder fell out. It was a cheap firearm, and the metal pin on which the cylinder turned had been snapped by the weight of the car.

Dropping the useless weapon, Doc whipped back to the post. The dangerous foray had been executed with his best speed, so swiftly that his foes had hardly perceived his move.

The plane engine caught with a *bang! bang!* and a moan. The four swarthy gunmen ceased shooting and piled into the craft. The ship began to scud, its tail lifting.

Without time for his engine to warm up, the pilot pulled off. It was his lucky day. The engine kept turning, and the black bat of a craft clubbed its way up into the moonlight.

Leveling off in the air, the black plane headed westward. Doc Savage watched it only long enough to make certain of the direction it was taking. Then he swung over and knelt beside the man who had gone under the sedan.

Life remained in the fellow; he was still moaning.

Doc grasped the man. To a bystander, the bronze man's manner might have seemed rough. But Doc knew what he was doing; he possessed a fund of surgical lore which was probably unequaled.

He straightened the victim out until he was more the shape of a human being. Then, using his flashlight, Doc examined him. An X ray would have helped; but he learned the important thing without it.

This man could not live long.

"Not a chance, fellow!" Doc told him. There was no use keeping it from him.

"Como dice?" The man's query was a wispy, tortured whisper. "What did you say?"

His hearing must have been damaged.

Instead of repeating the statement, Doc Savage put a question: "What's behind all this, hombre?"

The man's eyes only stared glassily. It was as if he had not heard.

"What are you fellows after?" Doc asked, his voice even louder.

The man's eyes seemed as crystal balls fixed in his head. Nothing came past his lips but labored, painful breathing.

"Who is your boss?" Doc persisted.

"Voy á casa!" said the man. "I am going home."

He was delirious. Strands were breaking in the already thin life thread which suspended him over the Infinite Abyss.

Doc Savage, seeking to draw something of value from the delirium, leaned close and shouted loudly: "Señor Corto Oveja!"

"Oveja!" gurgled the dying man. "Oveja—fool—easily tricked."

"Tricked by whom?" Doc shouted.

This query brought no response.

With the tips of sinewy, practiced fingers, Doc touched the various nerve centers in the broken body. His vast knowledge enabled him to alleviate pain in this fashion. Although even his surgical skill could not save this man's life, he might prolong the flow of information, such as it was.

"Ivory cube!" gulped the dying man.

"What?" Doc yelled.

"All square, and of ivory!" the fellow moaned in Spanish. "Must get it—worth many million pesos!"

Doc continued his dulling pressure on the nerve centers. It was probable that the man did not even know he was being spoken to. Whatever information that came would be incoherent and by chance.

"Rico hombres!" came the agonized whisper. "Rich men! Rich men it will make us! Skeletons under a rock—the ivory cube was gone! The galleon with the crew of skeletons, we cannot find it!"

Doc's bronze features remained composed, but he was about as near bursting with impatience as he ever got. The mutterings of this man only deepened the mystery.

The dying man said loudly and clearly: "Señor Oveja and his daughter are fools, and easily deceived. Alex Savage——"

And then the man died.

"But what did he mean?" Monk demanded. "An ivory cube—a galleon with a skeleton crew—skeletons under a ledge—and a lot of pesos! What a hash of information to try to make something out of!"

Doc Savage had assembled his five men, and they stood together in the darkness at the edge of town. It was well past midnight.

"Figuring it out is a swell job for Monk!" dapper Ham said in a jeering voice.

"What do you mean?" Monk asked innocently.

"Trying to dope it out would drive an ordinary man half-witted," Ham assured him politely. "You're safe."

"Meanin' I'm half simple, huh?" Monk growled pleasantly. He addressed his pig. "Habeas, this shyster don't like you and me. Whatcha say to that?"

"'T' hell with 'im!" said the pig—at least it sounded as if the pig had replied.

Ham dropped his sword cane and jumped a foot in the air. "For crying out loud!"

"Don't he look funny!" questioned the voice which seemed to come from the pig.

Ham caught on, then. He grabbed his sword cane, straightened, and made a pass at Monk.

Only by a frenzied leap did Monk escape. He retreated to safety, carrying his pet shoat.

"I didn't know Monk was a ventriloquist!" chuckled Long Tom, the electrical wizard. "He must have just picked it up!"

A pitiful groan escaped Ham.

Doc Savage had delayed his recital while the horseplay progressed. Their escapades rarely got so perilous but that Monk and Ham could have no spats. This was only Monk's latest scheme to insult the sartorially perfect Ham.

"Much of what the dying man said was incoherent," Doc

resumed. "But two fragments of the information were fairly significant."

Johnny, the skinny archæologist, took off his spectacles which had the magnifying left lens.

"Which were they?"

"The reference to money," Doc explained. "Once he mentioned a hundred million pesos! That must be the motivation —the loot the gang is after."

"A hundred million pesos!" Monk gasped from the adjacent darkness.

"It may not be that much," Doc pointed out. "The fellow was delirious. He may have spoken the first large figure that came to his wandering mind."

"The dying man tipped us to one thing we had already guessed," mumbled the big-fisted Renny. "Señor Oveja, the guy with the peach of a daughter, is being tricked."

"We're making headway!" said the sharp-tongued Ham. "Now, will some one kindly explain what was meant by an ivory cube, and skeletons under ledges and in boats?"

No one had an answer to that.

"We may see some action before we get it cleared up," Doc said dryly. "Let's set sail, brothers!"

"Where to?" Ham questioned.

"To see about our baggage," Doc told him.

Their luggage, they discovered, after a bit of reconnoitering, was locked in the freight room at the local depot. The night station agent not only refused to turn it over, but when he learned Doc's identity, ran for a Mounted Policeman. It seemed the agent had been advised that Doc was wanted for questioning in connection with the death of the conductor, Wilkie.

Doc glided to the locked freight room the instant the agent was out of sight. He had no implement other than the thin blade of a pocket knife, which Monk produced. But he got the lock on the freight-room door open in a bit less than a minute.

By the time the station agent returned with a Mounted Policeman, Doc and his men had lost themselves in the night, carrying their various pieces of luggage with them.

Ordinarily, Doc coöperated freely with the police, but just now he did not care to be delayed. These Mounted Police were thoroughgoing; they might jail him, despite his influence.

"Where are we going?" asked Ham, trying to balance both his sword cane and his luggage in his arms.

"To the place where this trouble seems to be coming from," Doc told him. "Alex Savage's estate!"

Chapter 10
CABIN OF MURDER

"All I can say is that we picked *some* spot for a vacation!" Ham wailed loudly and mournfully.

The time was somewhat past noon, the following day. The spot was in the neighborhood of Alex Savage's cabin.

"I've been in a lot of tropical jungles!" Ham continued dolefully. "But they were boulevards compared to this!"

Ham was a man who entertained little liking for getting close to nature. He heartily disapproved of all rough going. This was not because he could not stand hardship—Ham could take it. What Ham did dislike, though, was seeing his costly, well-tailored clothes torn off his back. Clothes were Ham's passion. He would forego anything—except possibly a fight—to remain sartorially perfect.

His present garments were rapidly becoming rags. His spirits were sinking accordingly. Ham had donned a nifty woodsman's outfit before starting on this hike. His Park Avenue tailor had told him it was the proper thing when he purchased it. Ham had known better at the time, but had failed to resist the well-tailored lines of the outfit.

"Doc, where's a camera?" Monk demanded loudly. "I want Ham's picture as he looks now! The newspapers would go for it!"

Ham glared indignantly.

The business of reaching Alex Savage's woodland retreat they had found to be no small task. Doc had searched for an airplane, but the only craft available had been an old two-seater biplane. Locating the owner shortly after dawn, Doc bought the decrepit ship outright.

By dint of howling and groaning like a dying thing, the old crate had proved it could take three of them off the ground at once.

Lack of landing fields near Alex Savage's cabin had been another obstacle. To complicate things, a thick fog had been sweeping in from the sea. It had taken three hours of flying to even locate Alex Savage's cabin. Once he had found it, Doc could discern no sign of life about the place.

Doc had been forced to land something like ten miles from the cabin, directly inland. Four trips had been necessary to carry his friends and their load of baggage.

Now, they had been fighting their way through the wilderness for some hours.

"Holy cow!" Renny boomed. "Do you reckon they ever got your telegrams into this country, Doc?"

"I understand the mail is brought up the coast by boat," Doc told him. "Telegrams would probably come in the same way."

"If we only had Doc's big plane!" Ham groaned.

The ship to which Ham referred was Doc's enormous speed plane, a bus capable of descending on land or water. This craft now reposed in Doc's hidden hangar on the Hudson River in New York City. With it, a landing on the little bay in front of Alex Savage's cabin would have been a simple matter.

Doc had not used the plane to fly to Canada simply because he wished to get away from speed and bustle during his vacation.

For some time they had been following a small river. This stream flowed at a terrific pace, a great flat, moaning green serpent which shook white spray off its back at frequent intervals.

The river, Doc had determined from the air, emptied into the tiny bay on the shores of which Alex Savage's large cabin stood.

"Look!" Doc said abruptly. He leveled an arm.

Fog was crawling through the brush like lazy smoke; the vapor lay like a gray mold on the sky, stifling sunbeams and making the day almost twilight. In the creamy illumination, the object which Doc indicated was barely discernible.

It was a fresh grave, marked by a cross.

As they drew nearer, it became apparent that the cross was ponderous, reaching above Doc's shoulders. It was of wood, roughly hewn.

"The grave is only a few days old," Long Tom offered.

They all walked around to get a look at the inscription on the cross, burned into it on a place where the wood had been chiseled flat.

ALEX SAVAGE

"My uncle!" Doc said sharply.

Silence wrapped the little group for some minutes. Their faces were grim. Discovery of the grave had been a shower of cold water on their spirits.

That Alex Savage was blood kin to their bronze chief, accounted for part of the gloom settling on the group. Ordinarily, they were inclined to sail grandly through all sorts of perils, taking the occurrence of a death as an unpleasant thing which was part of the game.

But this was different. For a little while, as they stood there, adventure seemed somewhat to lose its tang.

"Do you suppose———" Homely Monk made a vague gesture. "I wonder if the death was natural?"

No one replied.

"He had a daughter, Patricia Savage," Doc said at last.

The sartorially inclined Ham seemed to have forgotten both his ragged garments and his good-natured enemy, Monk.

"Let's move!" he muttered. "Graves always get my goat!"

They left their depressing find. The grave was on a level shelf of ground. The gray fog hung all around like waterlogged curtains. Doc surmised that the spot overlooked the sea, for the way soon dipped sharply downward, and they could hear the mushy splashing of waves.

They scrambled over rocks, shouldered through brush. Behind them, the river moaned, but they eventually left that sound behind.

The fog, growing more dense, swirled about the men like the clammy tentacles of some fabulous colossus. No birds sounded in the trees. There was no perceptible wind, but waves continued to make low splashings in the distance. The splashes came at regular intervals, and no doubt were the result of a ground swell. In the thick fog, these sounds might have been the shuffling steps of some spectral wanderer.

"I don't care a lot for this place!" Monk announced.

"We're getting near the cabin," Doc said.

Monk glanced up sharply. He wondered how Doc had learned that. He decided the bronze man had recognized landmarks.

The truth was that Doc's sensitive nostrils had caught certain faint odors—scents which the others had missed. Doc's olfactory organs were of almost animal keenness, for training them was a part of the daily exercise routine which he took unfailingly.

The vague odor which he had detected was mainly that of gasoline. Also, there were certain flower scents alien to the region, which probably came from a woman's dressing room. Too, there was the faint odor of wood smoke. The smoke tang was old—not such as would come from a blazing fire.

Within the next hundred yards, the cabin came in sight. The sumptuous nature of the rustic establishment created a sensation.

"Holy cow!" Renny ejaculated. "This is quite a place!"

Doc said sharply: "There's nobody here!"

Again the bronze man was voicing what his amazing senses had told him. His ears, sharp beyond those of an ordinary human, had detected no stirrings of life.

The front door of the cabin gaping open, they went in.

A man lay face up on the floor. A length of staghorn stuck upright from his chest—the hilt of a knife!

Gliding across the floor, Doc Savage studied the dead man. "An Indian!" he said.

Then he made a brief examination. "A half-breed, I should have said. He died, as near as can be told, about the time we were having all our troubles on the train."

Doc indicated the wrinkled condition of the dead man's lower garments.. "The fellow got soaked to the armpits just before his death. His clothes show plainly that they dried on his motionless body. That means they were wet when he was killed, and dried later."

Doc removed the beaded moccasins from the corpse. There was more than a spoonful of bright, clean sand in each slipper.

To the trousers on the corpse was sticking smears of an amber-colored, sticky gum. There was more gum on the lifeless fingers.

To the gum on the trousers clung bits of bark; and to the gum on the hands stuck, not only bark, but tiny feathers and lint.

If the gum and the stuff clinging to it informed him of anything, Doc Savage did not remark on the fact at the moment.

Long Tom, the electrical wizard, looking slightly more unhealthy and pale than usual, asked: "Who is he?"

Doc shook his head in a slow negative. He walked through the other rooms. Everywhere there was evidence of a thorough search—furniture ripped apart, bedding torn and scattered, rugs jerked up. The stuffed, snarling head of a bearskin rug had been chopped open.

"The cabin was searched twice," Doc announced after his scrutiny.

"Twice!" exclaimed skeleton-thin Johnny, puzzled. "How do you figure that?"

Moving into the kitchen, Doc indicated a smear on the floor. It resembled molasses which had been spilled, and had become as hard as glass. An overturned can near by showed where the stuff had come from. This can bore a varnish label.

"Look at the label," Doc advised. "Notice how long it requires for that varnish to dry."

After he had looked, the dapper Ham said: "Twelve hours."

"Exactly. It is now perfectly dry, but it was spilled during the search. That means the hunt occurred at least twelve hours ago."

Doc went into a bedroom. A gasoline lantern lay on the floor. Its fuel-reservoir base had been split open. The floor about the wreck of the lamp was wet with gasoline.

"You fellows know how fast gasoline evaporates," Doc said. "That gas was spilled less than an hour ago. The second search was more thorough. They even split open the lantern base."

Johnny adjusted his spectacles which had the magnifier lens.

"I've been noticing things, too," he announced. "The breed lying dead in the front room is a servant. I noticed clothes which would fit him. These were in a small room in the rear—obviously a servant's room. There were woman's garments in the room, too. That means he had a wife."

"She's a very large woman, too," Doc agreed. "Her clothes were big. She's an Indian, judging by the bright colors she affects. Apparently she and her husband were the only servants on the place."

"What about the daughter, Patricia?" Renny rumbled.

Doc did not reply immediately. He roved into a bedroom where feminine garments littered the floor. He ended his wandering at a wastebasket which had been overturned, and which had held—among other trash—crumpled cleaning tissues. These were the paper napkins young women use to remove facial creams.

Picking up one of these tissues, Doc crushed it between his sensitive, metal-hard fingers.

"It was used this morning," he said. "That means the young woman was present that recently."

"But where is she now?" Renny boomed. "And where is the fat servant?"

Renny was asking questions as if he thought his bronze chief had been present at whatever had happened here in the cabin. Renny knew from past experiences that Doc could come upon a scene such as this, and, because of his weird ability to read vague clews, get a story which came uncannily near being the truth.

"I'll show you," Doc said, thereby proving Renny had not been too optimistic.

Doc beckoned the group outdoors. He pointed to tracks in the soft earth. It had evidently rained at dawn, or shortly afterward. And distinguishable in the dirt were footprints of three men and two women. One of the women had worn moccasins, the other low-heeled, hobnailed boots.

"The two women have been kidnaped," Doc said bluntly.

The five aides swapped blank glances. How Doc could look at a set of footprints and tell there had been a kidnaping was beyond their deepest understanding.

Pointing, Doc said: "Notice the tracks show where one of the men shoved the girl—shoved her hard. It was no playful push. He would hardly have done that if the girl was going with them willingly."

Renny waved acknowledgment with his big hands. "You win, Doc."

"The kidnapers were our friends who escaped in the black monoplane," Doc continued.

The five men were fairly accustomed to this sort of thing—Doc's habit of plucking gems of information out of thin air. They had seen him do miracles on more than one occasion. But they could not help looking a bit stunned.

"Holy cow!" Renny rumbled. "I don't see how you can tell that, Doc."

"These tracks were made by the same men who attacked me when I started to follow the trail of luminous arrows from the train," Doc replied. "Those men were members of the gang who escaped in the plane."

He dropped to a knee and inspected the footprints more thoroughly. Then he reiterated: "I am sure of it! Not only the size, but certain worn patches on the soles exactly coincide."

"O. K., O. K.," Renny muttered. "All we need to know now is where the two women prisoners are being held."

"That will take some trailing," Doc replied.

The trail following was an easy matter for a few yards. Then, in the center of a great litter of rocks, the prints vanished. Nowhere could they be seen.

"They began leaping from rock to rock," Doc decided. "They can't do that forever. We'll circle."

Scattering, Doc and his men ranged the vicinity. They did not spread so widely but that they could hear each other call, however.

Shortly, Long Tom cried loudly: "Come over here, you guys! I ain't got the trail, but I've got something else!"

The unhealthy-looking electrical wizard was standing near a dense thicket of spruce. At his feet, brownish stains colored the rank woods grass.

"Blood!" he exclaimed dramatically.

"Thoroughly dried," Doc agreed after a close scrutiny. "Part of it was washed away by the rain last night."

The bronze man swung slowly around the spot, eyes on

the ground. Several times, he stopped and parted the grass.

The rain had washed away signs, leaving few that could be read. To eyes less than superbly trained, the stretch of forest presented absolutely no clew. Penetrating the spruce thicket, Doc spent some time in it.

He came out of the spruce and said: "In there was where the breed was murdered."

"Yeah?" Monk grunted.

"Maybe I should have said, *from* in there was where he was murdered. The knife must have been thrown. Signs show the breed came out here to meet some one. Evidently, whoever he was meeting got him with a knife thrown from the thicket."

"Any chance of trailin' the killer?" Renny demanded.

"No. The fellow was careful to follow rocky ground coming and going. The rain last night wiped out what few tracks he did make."

Monk had been inspecting the rain-faded prints around the bloodstain. Laboriously, he was finding the tracks which Doc had discovered almost at a glance.

"The two women evidently found the slain Indian," the homely chemist declared. "They carried him to the cabin. Here're the tracks. One set was made by boots, the other by moccasins."

Monk glanced over his shoulder. He wanted to see if Doc would verify the deduction. Monk started. His eyes flew wide.

Doc Savage was nowhere about!

Doc's five friends showed no excitement over the bronze man's disappearance. Doc had a disconcerting habit of vanishing on certain occasions. Doc had merely glided into the brush, of course, but his going had been so silent as to seem spectral.

By the time his absence was noticed, Doc had covered scores of yards. He traveled swiftly until he was a full quarter of a mile from the cabin. Then he swung in a wide circle.

The bronze man seemed to undergo a strange change. He became animallike in his searching for the trail. He utilized not only his eyes, but his sense of smell as well. Much of the time, he traveled on all fours. Occasionally, when desiring to move swiftly, or to clear a tangle of brush which no man could have penetrated without infinite labor, he sprang upward and swung along, with the prodigious agility of a monkey, from one tree limb to another.

It was a tangle of spider webs which finally showed Doc the trail.

The webs had been torn from their anchorage by some passing body, and hung dangling. A few yards from that point, Doc found a footprint. It was small; unmistakably feminine. He did not touch it, did not span its proportions with his fingers. But he knew it was the footprint of the girl who had been seized from the cabin.

It was somewhat uncanny, the ability, which Doc had acquired by long practice, to judge size by eye alone. Like Doc's other unusual accomplishments, there was nothing supernatural about this. It was an accomplishment perfected by his remarkable routine of exercises.

This routine occupied two hours daily, and in it was a process where he cast small white balls on the ground repeatedly, calculating just how far apart they had fallen. Careful measurements verified his judgment.

Doc followed the trail. It was not easy. The kidnapers had taken pains to conceal their path. They trod rocky ground wherever possible. They entered a small stream, followed it fully two hundred yards; here, water had washed away the tracks.

At one point—an eddy where the water was stagnant— Doc found a faint haze of mud still suspended. It had been stirred up by the passing of his quarry. This proved they were not far ahead.

Going became more difficult. The trail mounted sheer slopes, dived into rocky gulches. Stony boulders and ledges were steadily underfoot. The stuff would not retain footprints.

The wild western country produces certain individuals who are known as "sign readers." These are expert trackers, and are employed to trail thieves, find lost live stock, and kindred other jobs. So expert do these men become that they can look at a stretch of ground and see a clear trail where another man can distinguish nothing.

Had a sign reader been watching Doc Savage now, he would have been driven to conclude himself a veritable amateur. For it was in actuality no trail at all which Doc followed. The stony earth retained no prints.

Doc ranged back and forth, his strange golden eyes photographing everything in his mind's eye. He discerned certain bugs and small lizards loitering about the rocks. In other places, these were not in evidence. It was plain they had been frightened to cover.

They were such vague clews as this which guided the bronze giant.

The noise of the river became audible. The kidnapers seemed to be heading straight for the rushing torrent. The

noise of the river was like that made by a large tree being
shaken by some gigantic hand.

Wadded masses of fog crawled through the rocks like
enormous, gray phantom cats. In spots underfoot, little pud-
dles of water stood, the result of the rain of the night before.

Doc found where one of the party he was following had
stepped into a pool, and left a plain trail for some distance.
The boot tracks were small—those of the girl. A bit farther
on, Doc began finding small colored glass beads, of the
sort used in decorating Indian moccasins.

Both women seemed to be doing their bit to advertise
the trail.

The roaring of the river became louder. It might have been
a noisy beast drawing near. The sound had lost its likeness
to a tree being shaken. It was ugly and throbbing, and full
of sobs and gurgles. It had a quality of ugly savagery. It
caused the very eardrums, against which it battered, to ache.

Then Doc came to a canyon. It was perhaps a hundred
feet deep. He could not see the opposite walls, nor the bottom. He had to climb down to see how deep it was.

Upstream a few rods, there was a high waterfall. This
was making the roaring that hurt the ears.

The trail which Doc was following ended at the water's
edge. The waterfall made a vast thunder in the canyon, and
it was shattered into spray by its plunge over the precipice.
From the noisy inferno, mist arose like smoke from a burning house. It mingled with the fog; it darkened the sun. Its
wetness drooled on the surrounding rocks until they ran
rills of water, as if it were raining.

Doc lifted his gaze. Overhead, the mist clouds collided
and merged and tumbled like fighting things.

For perhaps a minute he stared upward. Then he lowered
his eyes. The river was all foam. Waves snapped twice the
height of his head. Their tops spat foam like ravenous
jaws.

Here and there a rock jutted from the stream bed. So
swift was the flood that air spaces were left behind these
rocks, which reached far down toward the stream bed.

By peering closely, Doc could discern the tracks of those
he was following. The party had waded directly out into the
boiling waters.

This was puzzling. No human being could wade the cur-
rent; no boat could exist in it.

Doc glanced upward again. The mist that lathered the air
overhead seemed to fascinate him. He watched it go through
convulsions for a bit. Then he clambered up the canyon side.

The walls were not exactly sheer, but they were steep enough that no loose rocks clung in mid-air. Fifty feet, Doc climbed—seventy-five. He was still in the clouds of spray. The stuff dashed against his face.

Pausing, he aligned himself with the tracks which had disappeared into the stream. He was a little to the right. He corrected his position. Then he looked upward.

Very low, yet penetrating the cataclysmic roar of the waterfall with seeming ease, came a tiny trilling note—the sound that was characteristic of Doc Savage. The fantastic note seemed hardly to come into being, then it was gone again. Doc himself showed no sign of being aware that he had made it.

The bronze man was studying what he had found. It was simply a rope tied securely to a tree. The rope stretched across the canyon.

Doc had expected something like this. It was the only thing that explained the tracks which had entered the stream. Some kind of a sling was pulled back and forth on this aërial cableway, he believed. The sling must hang low enough to enable those in the water to grasp it. The ingenious thing about this crossing device was that the cable stretched where it was completely hidden by clouds of mist and spray from the waterfall.

Doc grasped the cable and tested it. Then he leaped high in the air and landed, perfectly balanced on his feet, on the cable. He did not go hand over hand across the ropes, as another man might have done. He ran atop it, in the fashion of a tightrope walker.

Spray had made the rope very slippery. More treacherous footing would have been difficult to imagine. Doc seemed to give it no more consideration than he would have given a sidewalk. He carried no balancing rod—without which few tightrope walkers venture to perform—yet his balance was perfectly maintained.

The rope sagged in the middle, making the crossing more dangerous. Below, waves darted up like green-snouted, repellent lizards of titanic size. A fall meant certain death.

The rope curved sharply upward. Doc tilted far forward to maintain his balance, and his feet slipped repeatedly on the spray-wet fiber. These slippings, which would have raised the hair of a spectator, seemed to affect Doc's nerve not at all. He appeared to be as immune from fear as the metal he resembled.

A tree appeared in the misty void. To it was secured the rope end. Doc discerned a rude basket of sticks, pulleys, and ropes lying near by. It was a makeshift car for the cableway over the canyon.

Doc was almost on the point of leaping from the rope to solid ground when a man appeared beside the tree. He was squat, swarthy, and wore greasy coveralls. He had a rifle stock jammed against his shoulder.

The rifle coughed a tongue of flame which actually blackened the coat fabric over Doc's heart. The bullet made a tiny, ragged hole in the patch of powder-burned cloth.

Chapter 11

THE VANISHED BOX

Doc Savage's shoe soles seemed to acquire roller bearings. His giant form skittered back down the sloping wire.

He was bent nearly double now—he had folded into that position an instant after the rifleman fired. His movements were strangely grotesque. He slouched forward and seized the rope, his arms and legs whipping wildly! Doc seemed to be trying to retain his grip on the rope.

The swarthy rifleman leaned far out to peer through the mist.

"Bueno!" he hissed. "My bullets hit his heart!"

The man jacked a fresh cartridge into his rifle, planted the weapon against his shoulder, and aimed deliberately.

He could barely make out Doc's figure. It was a feverishly contorting, bronze-hued smear in the dripping gray abyss. The bronze man's movements reminded the rifleman of a squirrel that had been shot, and was attempting frantically to cling to its limb. Even as the man peered over his rifle sights, the metallic figure fell away from the overhanging cable.

Spray which boiled up from the water swallowed Doc's falling body.

"Bueno!" hissed the swarthy man again. He lowered his rifle. "He did not need a second shot."

The rifleman did not take the death of the bronze man for granted, however. He scrambled down the steep wall of the canyon to the water. There, washed by spray which the mad waters flung up, he explored.

He was positive Doc Savage had fallen into the river where it was roughest and running most violently, and equally sure Doc could not have escaped, even had he not been shot through the heart.

The man climbed back up the canyon wall and left the vicinity. He seemed none too familiar with the region. His progress was a series of careful sallies from one landmark to another. He stood near a tree, which had an extra large trunk, until he located a pair of large boulders which looked familiar. His next lap was to a brier thicket.

The fellow was plainly no woodsman, and he was taking no chances on getting lost.

He did not have far to go, soon entering a large grove of trees. There was a clearing in the center of the grove.

Four tents were pegged out in the clearing. The canvas was painted a green hue which camouflaged perfectly with the leaves overhead.

At the edge of the clearing stood an enormous, brushy-looking mound of green. This had a somewhat artificial look. However, only close examination would have revealed that the mound was made of freshly cut green boughs.

The boughs were stacked over a black monoplane, concealing it thoroughly. It would be almost impossible for an aviator flying over it to detect presence of the black ship.

Several men sprang to meet the bridge guard. They had rifles in their hands; revolvers were belted about their midriffs.

"Mulo cabeza!" gritted a man. "Mule head! You were left to guard the rope over the river!"

"Keep your shirts on, caballeros!" chuckled the rifleman. "What do you think I have just done?"

"Deserted your post!" somebody growled.

"No, amigo! I was standing at the rope end with my rifle ready, when the bronze man tried to cross. I shot him in the heart! He fell into the river!"

"Bueno!" chortled the other, suddenly delighted. "Good! Did he fall where the water ran swiftest?"

"He fell where no man could swim, amigo."

More men stumbled out of the green tents. They crowded around the man who was the self-admitted killer of Doc Savage. They were prepared to make a hero of the fellow.

"You are quite a caballero!" declared a man. "Many others have tried to kill this bronze wizard and failed. I once heard a rumor that he was gifted with everlasting life—that he could not be killed."

"Where did you hear that rumor, señor?" demanded a listener.

"In our native Spain, amigos."

"Tue?" ejaculated the other. "What? Has the fame of Doc Savage penetrated to our native land?"

"*Si, si!* That bronze man was known to many lands."

"*Was* is correct, señors," chuckled another fellow.

The late bridge guard swelled with pride. He flashed white teeth in an expansive grin, and stuck out his chest like a pouter pigeon.

"It is possible I shall draw a bonus when our boss hears of this, eh señors?" he queried.

"We must find the ivory cube before anybody draws a bonus!" one of the others reminded.

"Have you not yet learned where the white block is?" snapped the guard.

"What do you think we are—magicians?" snarled one of the group. "We have not had time to question the señorita —fittingly."

"The fat one—the squaw—she is what the Yankees call a bat from hell!" a man offered. He felt tenderly of an ear. From the upper end of the ear, a semicircular segment had been bitten. "Like a dog, the squaw snapped at me! Before I could dodge, she was spitting out a piece of my ear!"

Somebody unkindly laughed.

Five of these men were the fellows who had escaped in the black monoplane. The others—there were seven more— were somewhat incrusted with grease and dirt, an indication they had been encamped here in the wilderness for some time. The only clean, well-kept thing about them was their guns. These were spotless, freshly oiled, and carried in open holsters.

"What do we do next?" questioned a man.

"We will let our chief know that I have killed Doc Savage," said the rifleman who had guarded the rope bridge.

"Have you forgotten, my friend?" somebody chided him, "that we have strict orders never to go to our chief. He always comes to us."

"The chief, señors, should know what I have done," insisted the man. "It was no small feat! Here is how I did it!"

The man now proceeded to describe a terrific fight at one end of the rope bridge. Many blows had been exchanged; bullets had flown, and knives had flashed—to hear him tell it.

The fellow was an accomplished liar. Out of his imagination, he conjured an amazing battle; before he had finished talking, he had not only slain Doc Savage, but had first bested the bronze giant in a physical contest.

"And that is how it happened, hombres!" The tale spinner wiped perspiration from his forehead. The sweat had been brought out by the very fierceness of the combat which he had just described. "Truly, it was the great fight of my life."

"You are *mucho hombre!*" a listener agreed, tongue in his cheek. "If you could now lead us to the galleon with the crew of skeletons, you would indeed be a hero."

"Si, si," agreed the world's champion liar. "The galleon of skeletons! We will find it, amigo! But the ivory cube comes first!"

The words caused the men to exchange glances. An ugly determination rode each face. Here was a question on which they all seemed to be of the same mind.

"A man should go and guard the river crossing," some one suggested.

"Not me, señor!" snapped the man who had lately been at the post. "I have done my guardings for this day."

This struck the others as being a reasonable statement. So another man was dispatched to take a position at the rope over the river.

"Now to question the Señorita Savage," the leader announced.

They moved in a body to one of the green tents.

"Come out, Señorita Savage!" commanded the leader.

There was no response from the tent.

"Come, señorita!" the man directed, more sharply.

Once more, nothing happened.

The man stooped and looked in. He emitted a surprised yell. He dived into the tent like a terrier after a rat. There was noise as he jumped about, and two blankets flew outdoors.

"Es no posible!" the man screeched. "It is not possible! Señorita Savage is gone!"

Had the men suddenly discovered that they were standing over a lighted charge of dynamite, they could not have scattered more quickly. In a wild wave, they spread around the tent. At the rear wall, one fellow found a stake loose.

"Here is where she escaped!" he cried.

"En verda!" sneered the former bridge guard. "Indeed! So this is the way you hombres keep track of your prisoners!"

"Your own big mouth is to blame, caballero!" some one advised him angrily. "While you were talking so loud and fast, telling us what you did to this man Savage, she escaped!"

"Scatter, hombres!" shouted the man who seemed to possess some semblance of authority. "Look everywhere for her! She cannot have gone far."

Like a pack of hounds which had lost a trail, the men dispersed. Some dashed madly into the woods; others peered in brush clumps. There was plenty of shrubbery, for the gang had not troubled to clear the camp site.

Some of the men probed about the camp. One of these went to the green tent which held the squaw, Tiny. A single glance inside sufficed to show that the squaw's legs were still bound securely. The man started to back out.

"Wait!" grunted Tiny. "You want know what way white gal go?"

"*Si, si, señorita!*" said the man. "Yes, yes!"

"Cut um loose," said Tiny. "Me tell um."

"*Si!*" exclaimed the man delightedly. He sprang inside. He was hardly in the tent when a slender, sinewy brown arm enwrapped his throat from behind. This caused his mouth to fly wide open. Another brown hand promptly stuffed a wadded handkerchief between the gaping jaws.

Patricia Savage had been crouching to one side of the tent door while Tiny enticed their victim inside.

During the excitement which had attended the arrival of the killer, Patricia had managed to free herself and crawl into the tent which sheltered the squaw.

Her escape had been discovered at an inopportune moment. Given a few seconds more, and Patricia would have been gone, along with Tiny.

Tiny reared up to help subdue the man. She gave a wrench, and the rope fell off her wrists. A kick, and her ankles were free. The ropes had merely been arranged to look like they were tied. That was Patricia's idea.

The man was probably not more than twenty-five, and quite husky. He had a neck like a young bull. He was more than a match for nine out of ten run-of-the-street men.

Patricia, however, had taken him by surprise. Moreover, she was a young lady who combined good looks with a well-developed muscle. She not only kept the man from yelling an alarm, but she had his wind completely shut off.

The man kicked, struck backward. Not for nothing had Patricia taken fencing lessons in a finishing school. She evaded his blows easily. The man grabbed her attractive bronze hair and gave it a tremendous yank.

Tiny went into action. Stooping, she seemed to pick something off the floor and plant it forcibly on the man's chin. It was a beautiful haymaker.

The man stopped struggling as suddenly as if he had been shot through the brain.

"Me learn that practicing on Boat Face," Tiny muttered. A moment after she had spoken, Tiny seemed to remember that Boat Face was dead. Her lower lip quivered, and tremendous sobs shook her enormous bosom.

Patricia eyed their unconscious victim, then appraised the squaw's size.

"I'll have to put on his clothes and walk out of camp," she said. "If they would fit you, I'd let you go, Tiny. But you're too darn big. When I get out of camp, I'll make a fuss. I'll yell or something. When they rush to investigate, you beat it."

"O. K.," said Tiny.

The man had a gun. Patricia took that; then she yanked off the man's shirt. After this, she turned her back.

When she wheeled around again, Tiny had the fellow's pants and shoes, and had spread a blanket over his sleeping form.

Patricia now donned the garments. She picked up the man's hat, looked at the greasy interior, grimaced, scrubbed it vigorously with her elbow, and put it on. She stuffed her bronze hair under it.

"How do I look?" she asked Tiny.

Tiny leaned over and popped their prisoner on the jaw with a fist. He had shown signs of reviving. "You look all right, Miss Pat."

Patricia calmly walked out of the tent and strolled for the woods. If any of her enemies discovered her, there was a good chance that they would start shooting. They were of a race notoriously quick on the trigger.

No one, fortunately, saw through her disguise. When she reached the first trees, Patricia resisted an impulse to run. The woods were full of maddened searchers.

Patricia had not covered two rods when she saw a human hunter. He was prowling around, peering this way and that. It chanced that he was the same individual who had been guarding the bridge.

Patricia, peering out of her tent while making her escape, had seen this man. She had heard him bragging of the murder he had committed. The name of the murder victim had been a shock.

It was Patricia's first knowledge that her famous cousin, Doc Savage, was in the vicinity.

The young woman was at a loss to explain why Doc was in this part of Canada. She did not know it, but she had not received the bronze man's messages advising her of his northern vacation.

Patricia had intended to send to Doc for help. But that morning, she had found both the storage barrel and the launch tanks empty of gasoline. This had prevented her from going to send a telegram. She was relieved that no gesture of hers had drawn Doc to his death.

However, Patricia was horrified to think that Doc had perished. She was also filled with a consuming rage against his killer.

Patricia was no butterfly who blossomed forth only at social functions. That did not mean she was a wall-flower when confronted with the glittering pomp of society. But at the same time, she was a two-fisted young woman who could go out and do things.

Glaring at the self-admitted murderer of Doc Savage, she made a decision. She concluded to seize the fellow and turn him over to the nearest Mounted Policeman.

Stepping behind a tree, Patricia drew her gun—the weapon she had taken from the man she had overpowered. She examined it; the thing was loaded. She waited purposefully.

Patricia could hear her victim approaching. He had been headed in this direction when she first saw him. She believed his course would take him within arm's length of the tree behind which she stood. In this, she was not wrong.

The man rounded the tree. He was looking in another direction, so his back was half turned. He did not see Patricia.

Reaching out, Patricia jammed the barrel of her gun against the nape of the man's neck.

The man gave one horror-stricken scream and fell over in a dead faint.

Patricia was thunderstruck. She would have maintained that it was beyond the most nervous of women to faint at the mere touch of cold metal on the back of a neck. But what Patricia had no means of knowing was that this man was highly wrought up.

For the last half hour, the fellow had been seeing Doc Savage in his mind's eye. Especially did he remember the metallic quality which was Doc's chief characteristic.

When cold metal touched his neck, his reaction was that Doc's frosty ghost had seized him. So he fainted.

"Darn it!" snapped Patricia, and began running deeper into the woods.

By yelling before he had keeled over, the man had upset her plans. The howl had spread the alarm.

"Que hay!" shouted a man from somewhere. "What is the matter?"

Patricia hoped he would be a long time finding out. She put on more speed, and began to have a faint hope that she would make it. If she did, her plan would have worked out to a nicety. The alarm would be exactly what was needed to give Tiny her chance to escape.

Patricia was too optimistic, however. A man hurled himself from behind a tree into her path. His gun was in its holster. With bare hands, he sought to seize the fleeing girl.

The fact that the man was not using his gun saved his life. Instead of shooting him, as he no doubt deserved, Patricia made a pass at his head with her revolver barrel.

Clank! went the gun on the fellow's skull. He fell at her feet.

Thinking he was unconscious, Patricia started to step over him. But the man grasped her by the ankles and tripped her.

Too late, Patricia sought to shoot him—through a leg. They scuffled for a moment. Then Patricia lost her revolver.

That marked the finish. In a moment, more swarthy men came rushing through the timber to the aid of their comrade. Seizing Patricia, they bound her hand and foot. Then they carried her back to camp.

The first thing Patricia saw in camp was the voluminous Tiny. The squaw lay on the ground in an attitude of slumber.

"What have you done to her?" Patricia shrieked.

A man tapped his rifle barrel expressively and said: "I kees her weeth thees, señorita."

Patricia gripped her upper lip between firm white teeth, and said nothing. She was worried and angry enough to burst into tears. She felt certain she would not get another such opportunity to escape.

"What do you want with me?" she demanded of the men.

"We have told you that, señorita!" one said.

"The ivory cube?" Patricia asked bitterly.

"Si, señorita. The ivory cube is right. We want it."

"It'll be a long old day before you get it!" Patricia retorted angrily.

The man shrugged his shoulders and made expressive hand-spreading gestures.

"Quien sabe?" he smiled coldly. "But why are you so determined not to give it to us?"

"I'll never turn the cube over to my father's murderers!" Patricia rapped.

The young woman's captor looked hurt at this. His face assumed an injured expression. He shrugged several times.

"But, señorita," he said mournfully, "you do us *mucho* wrong to think that."

Patricia sniffed indignantly.

"Of course, I have no proof," she said. "You could claim the werewolf did it."

The man gave a pronounced shiver. He rolled his eyes skyward. He crossed himself.

"Heaven forbid!" he muttered. "The werewolf, señorita —has he bothered you also?"

Patricia eyed the man narrowly. She could not for the life of her tell whether he was putting on an act for her benefit, or telling the truth.

"Oh, don't try to kid me!" she said finally.

"We are not kidding anybody, señorita. We know nothing of this murder. But we do know you have a certain ivory cube. It is imperative that we have it. We are going to get it."

"Why do you want it?" Patricia countered.

"That, señorita, is our own affair!"

"I examined the block," Patricia said wonderingly. "There is no inscription of any kind on it. It seems perfectly solid —it does not ring hollow when you tap it. Of what possible value can a plain ivory block be to you?"

"So you *do* have the block!" her captor exclaimed triumphantly.

Patricia bit her lips. The cat had been in the bag without her knowing it, and she had let it out.

Her captor waved his arms in excitement. He shouted loudly to his fellows: "You hear, amigos? She has the block! We have but to make her tell where it is!"

The swarthy men gathered about. Eying them, Patricia decided they were about as evil-looking a collection as she had ever seen. Any one of them would have drawn a second look from a policeman. She did not like the fierce greed on their ugly faces.

The men began to make cruel suggestions.

"A knife on her pretty face!" proposed one. "That will make her talk!"

"*Si, si,*" agreed another. "But a red-hot iron is better."

"Why not work on the squaw?" asked one man. "I think the Señorita Savage is a young woman who will talk to save her servant."

At this point, the man who had fainted when he felt Patricia's cold gun against the back of his neck, regained consciousness. He glanced about in a dazed fashion, keeping silent until he found out what was going on.

"What happened to you?" somebody asked him.

"She struck me over the head!" replied the wily liar. "But, at great risk to my life, I managed to yell the alarm!"

A man ran up. He carried a small portable gasoline stove of the type woodsmen sometimes use—usually tenderfoot woodsmen who have trouble building fires.

He pumped up the pressure tank on the stove, and applied a lighted match. The stove began to roar softly, and give out an intensely hot blue flame.

The man placed the stove near Tiny. Then he prepared to

grasp the squaw's feet and hold them over the blue flame.

He had almost forced the feet into the flame when there was a loud crash. The gasoline stove lost much of its shape, and jumped end over end. It had been hit by a large rock, flung with terrific force.

The swarthy men whirled.

They saw a sight which, to a man, they carried in their memories to their day of death.

Chapter 12

THE HAND THAT BECKONED

Had an elephant walked out in that clearing in the Canadian woods, consternation could hardly have been greater. Certainly, the shock would have been less.

The late bridge guard shrieked loudly, spun around, and fled! His wild terror would have been comical, had it not been so harshly real. The man was stricken with horror.

He had seen a ghost coming across the clearing. A ghost of the bronze giant he had sent into the torrent below the waterfall! More appalling, this ghost was not moving with the stately walk usually attributed to its kind. The thing was coming with a speed which in itself seemed beyond human ability.

A towering bronze Nemesis, Doc Savage bore down on the swarthy man.

Doc's escape had been managed quite simply. He now wore the remarkable vest of many pockets which held his assortment of apparatus. This was lined with a metallic mail which would stop even a big-game rifle slug.

In one of the vest pockets was a long, slender, very strong silk cord. To the end of this was fixed a grappling hook.

Doc had simply hooked the grapple over the rope spanning the river, then lowered himself until he hung concealed in the clouds of spray boiling above the water. It chanced that the wait was almost his undoing, however. In the terrific roar of the falls, he had not heard his enemy descending the canyon side. Luckily, Doc had seen the other first.

Doc had climbed back up his silk cord to the cable, and swung hand-over-hand to terra firma.

The bronze man had followed his assailant to camp, and had been lurking near by ever since. Unfortunately, he had not been in a position to help Patricia with her escape. Her flight had been opposite Doc's place of concealment.

Doc had demolished the gasoline stove with the thrown rock.

What now transpired happened with the violence of exploding dynamite and the rapidity of an electrical phenomena.

Patricia Savage had often wondered what her famous cousin looked like. She had read of some of his feats. She had heard tales of him. But she had never met Doc, and she had doubted his being the man he was said to be.

Watching Doc in action, Patricia concluded he was all he was rumored to be, and then some. Discounting the fellow who had fled, there were eleven men in the clearing. All were fair physical specimens. Moreover, they were armed.

One man sprang forward, leveled his revolver at Doc's chest, and pulled the trigger repeatedly. The range was short. He could hardly miss. It was possible to count the ragged holes which his bullets caused to appear magically in the bronze man's coat front.

Doc did not waver. The slugs might have been beans pelted at a rhino. He came on like a juggernaut of metal.

The gunman finished shooting, and threw his revolver wildly at Doc.

The bronze man dodged. The way he did this was in itself reason for popeyed surprise. The gun seemed to pass through flesh and bone, so swiftly did he weave his head aside and back.

"I shoot him six times!" shrieked the one who had thrown the gun. "He should be dead!"

The seeming impossibility of what they had just witnessed held the others spellbound. The fractional moment during which they stood and stared proved disastrous.

The mighty bronze man drove a hand inside his clothing, brought out a small metal egg of an object. He flung it.

The metal lump dropped among the swarthy men with a loud report!

Without exception, the men clapped hands over their eyes. They began to yell in terror. They could see nothing—the world had suddenly gone jet black!

They were either too stupid or too surprised to realize they were now standing in a smoke cloud—a great wad of inky blackness which had spread with lightning suddenness from the metal egg.

Patricia Savage was only slightly less surprised than her captors. She was lifted and borne rapidly through the black cloud. With such uncanny ease was she carried that Patricia was slow to realize human hands were bearing her.

She could not see a thing in the almost blue-black void, but she knew it must be the gigantic bronze man who was bearing her.

Patricia was carried out of the smoke. The day, dim and vaporous as it was, seemed almost brilliant after the sooty pall out of which they had come.

The young woman discovered her eyes had not been affected by the dense smoke. They did not smart.

She was lying across the bronze man's mighty shoulders, she discovered.

Patricia looked down and gave a violent start. Under one arm, as easily as another man would carry a sack of groceries, Doc had tucked Tiny. The squaw weighed well over two hundred pounds.

Doc Savage whipped across the clearing, his great speed seemingly impeded not at all by his burdens. Patricia found it hard to believe. This metallic giant had the strength of a dozen men!

Reaching the edge of the clearing, Doc planted the two women on their feet.

"Run!" he said, and pointed in the direction of the rope spanning the river gorge.

Patricia began: "If you need any help——"

"Do what I say!" Doc said sharply.

Patricia looked slightly indignant, but began running.

Turning to the right, Doc veered around the clearing edge. His progress was swift, but he also zigzagged from side to side, keeping behind brush and trees as much as possible.

None of the swarthy men had come from the black cloud as yet. This was probably because the somber pall had spread until it was more than a hundred feet across. The smoke boiled like a dark foam.

One of the men finally staggered into view. He stood staring stupidly at the fog-packed sky, as if it were something he had never expected to see again.

Suddenly, he understood the nature of what he had thought to be a weird blindness. Drawing his revolver, he fired it rapidly into the air.

"This way, hombres!" he screeched. "We have been tricked!"

In his excitement, the man failed to observe a bronze apparition which streaked under the pile of green boughs that covered the black monoplane.

The instant he was concealed under the brush, Doc

glanced back to see if he had been observed. Apparently he was unseen.

He was under the right wing of the plane. Doc crawled to the big radial motor, and his deft fingers explored its innards.

Doc's familiarity with airplane motors was as profound as his other lines of knowledge. He had, in fact, designed a motor which was in use on a large air line in the United States. This was not public knowledge, it being popularly supposed that the motor was the work of an elderly and kindly inventor whom Doc had befriended. Nor did any one but the inventor, who was also the manufacturer, know that the design for the motor had saved the old gentleman's business.

The motor of this black plane was fitted with two carburetors. Doc removed both, his corded fingers loosening the fastener nuts after a little straining. Fortunately, they were not tight.

Doc buried both carburetors under the plane, carefully replacing the dirt so that the hiding place would not be noticed.

Peering through the fur of brush which camouflaged the ship, Doc saw the swarthy men. They were in a group, and heading for the opposite side of the clearing. A moment later, veering behind the immense wad of inky smoke, they were lost to view.

Doc Savage promptly deserted the plane. Entering the timber, he circled widely.

Patricia and Tiny had been running with all the speed they could muster. Patricia gave a start of surprise when Doc Savage materialized like a phantom beside her.

"One of those men shot right at you!" she gasped wonderingly. "I saw the bullets hit! Why didn't they harm you?"

"Bullet-proof vest!" Doc explained cryptically.

Many things were puzzling Patricia. Speaking as she ran, she sought to get them straightened out.

"You *are* Doc Savage, aren't you?" she asked.

"Right," Doc admitted.

"How does it happen you are here?"

"Better save the breath for running," Doc told her.

Patricia gasped with faint indignation. The fact that her father was a fairly wealthy man had not exactly spoiled her, but she was not accustomed to being told what to do in such short fashion.

"But," she snapped, "I want to know what——"

"There're lots of things we both want to know!" Doc told her. "We can save them until we get clear."

Patricia seemed about to express an opinion contrary to

this. But a loud, fierce shout from behind caused her to change her mind.

"*Buenos!*" was the cry. "Here is the trail!"

"Darn it!" cried Patricia, and saved her breath for running.

They reached the rope which spanned the gorge below the falls. The canyon was like a great caldron in which water boiled thunderously and poured up frost-cold steam.

Patricia glanced over the brink and shuddered.

"I was never so scared in my life as I was when they hauled me over in this thing," she declared, indicating the rickety cage which could be pulled across the rope.

Doc was somewhat at a loss to know why the swarthy men had spanned the river in this fashion. He put a question to clear that up.

"I presume there is no other point near by where the river can be crossed?" he asked.

"Not for miles in either direction," Patricia replied.

She peered over the brink once more, and watched bucketfuls of spray being flung higher than the canyon walls by the force of the torrent.

Patricia had been under a great strain for the last few hours. The thought of crossing this ominous chasm was the last straw. Her grip on her nerves slipped.

She clapped her hands tightly to her eyes and shrieked: "I won't go over! I can't!"

Doc reached for her. There was no time to be lost.

Patricia struck at him hysterically, shrieked again.

The young woman realized what she was doing, and was not at all proud of her performance. Nevertheless, she could not help it. She had a bad case of what is generally called the jitters.

She felt herself seized. One of the bronze man's hands glided past her cheek and pressed a certain spot near the cranial nerve center. There was a slight tingling sensation, and Patricia suddenly found herself powerless to move a muscle. It was weird.

She was tossed lightly across Doc's shoulders. Then the mighty bronze man seemed to leap outward, straight into the caldron below the falls. However, his feet landed on the rope, and he came to a perfect balance. He glided along the hemp strands.

During any one of the dozen seconds which followed, Patricia would have died cheerfully. It was the most ghastly interval of her existence. She had admired the work of circus performers in the big top—trapeze and tight-wire artists who did amazing things. But she had never seen a feat which equaled this bronze man's seemingly unconcerned defiance of death.

Patricia was placed safely on her feet on the opposite side. Doc's bronze fingers found nerve centers again. The young woman recovered use of her limbs magically.

Patricia knew enough of human anatomy to comprehend some of the enormous skill which lay in Doc Savage's fingers. She crouched on the edge of the cliff, dazed. She was frankly ashamed of herself.

Doc Savage crossed back over the chasm, running lightly on the rope.

Tiny was waiting there. She gazed into the chasm and shuddered.

"Wait!" she grunted uneasily. "Me take um chance—stay on this side."

The voluminous Tiny never was exactly sure what happened after that. The bronze hands pressed her head. She became helpless. Then she, also, was borne out over the thundering abyss.

Doc seemed to handle the squaw's weight as easily as he had managed Patricia's.

Safely across, he loosened the pulley from the anchor tree, and let the rope fall back into the torrent. This blocked pursuit.

Patricia had said that, for several miles, there was no other way of crossing the violent little river.

Doc Savage's five men greeted their chief noisily when he appeared. They were no little impressed by the exquisite beauty of Patricia Savage.

"Look at that bronze hair!" Monk breathed ecstatically in an aside. "Say, she might almost be Doc's sister!"

"She's a knockout for looks!" agreed the debonair Ham, forgetting himself so much as to agree with Monk.

"Back to the cabin," Doc directed. "We've got some talking to do."

Doc had encountered his aides some distance from the cabin. They retraced their steps to the structure.

Out of courtesy to the young woman, Doc unfolded his part of the story first. He began with the fake telegram on the train, and omitted few details.

"To sum up," he finished, "the whole thing is pretty baffling. The gang who just kidnaped you seem to be after an ivory block. And in some fashion, they must have learned we were coming here on a visit."

"They probably learned that by robbing the mail box," Patricia Savage suggested.

"That would explain it," Doc agreed. "They attacked me on the train in an effort to prevent me coming here. Then there's Señor Corto Oveja, his daughter, and El Rabanos. They headed in this direction, although we have seen no signs of them being around here."

"What part do they play?" Patricia asked.

"That's more mystery," Doc told her. "They were attacked on the train. They laid it onto me. And their assailants left one of those werewolf marks."

Patricia shuddered violently. "The werewolf marks! I have found several of them around this cabin."

"We saw one on the cabin floor," Doc admitted.

"Yes. That one appeared when I found Boat Face and Tiny afflicted with that weird sleep."

Doc and his men exchanged glances. They had by no means forgotten their own experience with the weird slumber. But what the fantastic affliction was, they had not yet learned.

"When did this all start?" Doc asked Patricia.

"Some weeks ago. My father found a prowler in our cabin. The fellow fled. A little later, a mysterious voice called from the woods and demanded that dad hand over the ivory cube. Dad refused——"

"What ivory cube?" Doc interjected.

"One father found on a rock ledge near here," Patricia replied. "Several human skeletons lay around the little block. It was years ago when he found it."

Speaking rapidly, the young woman told of the repeated demands for the ivory trinket.

"Then my father was found—dead!" she finished jerkily. "Doctors said his heart had gone back on him. I think he was murdered—a victim of that fantastic sleep."

Doc Savage indicated the lifeless figure of Boat Face. "When did that happen?"

"Last night, sometime," Patricia said slowly. "Tiny and I found his body this morning, just before the rain. We carried it to the cabin. A few minutes later, those swarthy men came and seized us. They took us by surprise."

"You haven't the slightest idea why the ivory cube is in demand?" Doc questioned pointedly.

"No."

"Let's have a look at it."

"Of course!" Patricia went to the bark-sheathed pillar which supported the living-room ceiling. She pressed a concealed catch, and the door flew open.

She shoved a hand confidently inside, and groped around. Then she bent over and stared into the recess.

"It's gone!" she gasped.

"Did Boat Face know where the cube was hidden?" Doc asked. His remarkable voice was smoothly unexcited, and told nothing.

"Yes," Patricia admitted.

"And he could have removed it without your knowing it?"

Patricia hesitated. As yet, she had no knowledge of the half-breed's duplicity.

"He could have," she admitted. "But I would rather think he did not take it. No doubt he heard a prowler, went to investigate, and was knifed."

"Boat Face—him no good!" said Tiny, with scant consideration for her dead husband. "Him no mean. Him just weak. And him foxy."

"Boat Face was killed at a secret meeting," Doc declared.

"How do you know?" Patricia asked.

"There were tracks."

"I didn't see any tracks!"

"They were there," Doc assured her. "I'm sorry, Pat, but Boat Face seems to have been a crook."

Patricia nodded slowly. She felt an agreeable tingling. Doc Savage had called her "Pat." This seemed to indicate that he had accepted her as one of the gang. Patricia was pleased.

"I don't know who took the ivory block," she said. "This thing is getting more involved all the time."

Doc Savage now made a second survey of the cabin and its vicinity. This search was so intense that it made his earlier hunt seem but a careless glance in comparison.

From a pack, which he had carried to this wilderness retreat, he removed what looked like a pair of tiny binoculars mounted in spectacle frames. The lenses of these were extremely powerful, and adjusted for a short distance.

Doc's unaided eyes were keen. But, wearing these eyeglasses, he could cover the ground with microscopic thoroughness.

It was around the boathouse that his scrutiny became most intensive. In addition to the launch, the boathouse contained several canoes. There was also a rack of holding spades, saws, axes, and other tools.

Doc studied one of the spades closely.

"Has this been used recently, Pat?" he asked.

Patricia thought it over before she answered.

"No," she said, "I'm quite sure it hasn't."

Lifting down the canoes one at a time, Doc examined them. Especially did he concentrate on the floor boards. On one of these he found a semicircular scar. When he tried the tip of the spade, it exactly fitted the mark.

Doc laid the spade aside.

Patricia picked it up, examined it. To her astonishment, she found nothing.

"I don't understand!" she said, puzzled.

Johnny came forward hastily, removing his glasses which had the magnifying lens. He let the young lady inspect the spade under magnification.

"Oh!" Patricia ejaculated. "This spade has been used recently to dig in sand! There are tiny scratches which are not a bit rusted."

Inspecting further, Doc found where a canoe had been carried to the water. The canoe had been floated to an out-of-the-way spot under some overhanging brush. There was no reason why it should be used for a regular point of launching. Yet marks in the sand showed that the canoe had arrived and departed numerous times. All of the tracks had been made by Boat Face's moccasins.

Doc noticed that bushes prevented the landing place from being seen from the cabin.

"Boat Face seems to have made numerous excursions!" he announced.

Patricia stared at Tiny. "Did you know about his trips?"

The squaw shrugged stoically. "Me sleep sound! Me not hear!"

Doc collected his men before the door of the cabin.

"Let's get organized," he said.

Doc's five aides brightened visibly at the words. So far, they considered themselves as having been rather useless. At least once in each adventure, Doc usually had occasion to make use of the particular talent which each of his men claimed.

Monk, the chemist, was first to receive orders.

"Got your portable laboratory?" Doc asked him.

The question was hardly necessary. Monk was rarely to be found far from his remarkable outfit of chemicals. This piece of equipment was wonderfully compact, yet Monk could do work with it which called ordinarily for a great outlay of equipment. Monk was something of a Houdini with the test tubes.

"I've got it," he said.

"I want you to go to work on the inside of the cabin," Doc told him. "Analyze and test everything."

Monk did not comprehend fully.

"But what will I look for?" he demanded.

"Anything that might give a clew as to what caused the weird sleep," Doc explained.

"I get you, Doc."

"Renny," Doc said; "think you can find our plane?"

Renny flicked an enormous hand inland. "Sure! I remember the way we came."

"You have a small mapping camera in your luggage, haven't you?"

"A special mapping lens which fits our regular camera," Renny said. "It amounts to the same thing."

"O. K.," Doc told him. "I want aërial photos of the vicinity of this cabin. Cover the region for several miles up and down the coast. Take one set of photos at a height of about five hundred feet. Take the others from a much higher altitude, at least a mile."

"Got you!" boomed Renny.

Patricia's pretty face was frankly incredulous.

She exclaimed, "You can't get pictures in this fog!"

"We use cameras equipped to utilize infra-light," Doc told her. "Haze and fog don't faze these infra-rays."

Renny gathered his equipment together and moved off, a giant of a man who was made to look smaller than he was by the incredible hugeness of his hands.

Doc Savage now addressed Long Tom and Johnny.

"You two fellows will work at the same job, but using different methods," he advised. "Long Tom, I want you to take electric-wave tests that will help to determine the possible presence of oil or deposits of mineral underground. Johnny will prospect outcroppings in search of anything that might be valuable. We, of course, are hunting for whatever this gang is after."

The two men lost no time getting busy. Few living men knew more of the earth's structure than did Johnny; if there were mineral outcroppings, the gaunt geologist with his manifying-lens spectacles could find them.

The electrical device which Long Tom would use, employed several principles known to scientific oil prospectors and others. Wave impulses, both sonic and electric, were sent into the earth. Their subsequent reaction betrayed any unusual subterranean formation.

"What about me?" Ham demanded.

"You will guard Miss Patricia," Doc said.

The rather handsome Ham grinned widely at this.

Homely Monk, who had overheard, emitted a loud groan. If there was anything Monk hated, it was seeing Ham enjoying himself in the company of an attractive girl.

Disgusted with the latest developments, Monk turned away to conduct his chemical experiments.

Chapter 13

AN OFFER

It was mid-afternoon of the following day. Things were pretty much at a status quo. Nothing had happened; nothing had been discovered that was of value. And it was still foggy.

Renny was off continuing his mapping, using the old plane. Johnny and Long Tom were still prospecting. They had found nothing the day before.

Monk was dividing his time between scowling at Ham, who was enjoying himself entertaining Patricia, and dabbling with his chemical equipment.

Doc Savage was just completing his exercise routine. He had been at it without pause for two hours. From the cradle, he had never missed a day of this ritual.

They were unlike anything else in the world, those exercises. Doc's father, a great surgeon and adventurer, had started him taking them. They were solely responsible for Doc's amazing physical and mental powers.

He made his muscles pull one against the other, straining until a fine film of perspiration covered his mighty bronze body. He juggled a number of a dozen figures mentally, extracting roots, multiplying, dividing.

In a small case, Doc carried an apparatus which made sound waves of frequencies so high and low that an ordinary ear could not detect them. Through a lifetime of practice, Doc had perfected his hearing to a point where the sounds were audible. He named several score of different odors after a quick olfactory test of small vials racked in the case which held his exercising equipment.

He read pages of Braille printing—the writing for the blind, which consists of tiny upraised dots. He did this as rapidly as another would peruse ordinary type. This attuned his sense of touch.

The whole exercise routine was pushed with an unbounded vigor. Five minutes at the clip would have prostrated an ordinary man—and an ordinary man would have found it impossible to do most of the work.

Monk came outdoors to get a breath of air. The chemical

analysis he was conducting at the moment was giving off a most unpleasant odor.

The sight of Ham and Patricia together seemed painful to Monk. He turned his gaze away, letting it rove the brush surrounding the cabin. Suddenly, his little eyes almost popped from their sockets.

Monk emitted a yell! The howl had tremendous volume. It scared birds off their limbs almost a mile away.

"A hand!" Monk bawled.

Ordinarily, Monk's voice was small, weak as a baby's. But it underwent a startling change when he was excited. It became tremendous, bawling, and made even Renny's thunder seem puny by comparison.

As he shouted, Monk pointed with both hands.

The others followed his gesture. They saw—nothing!

"What is it?" Patricia gasped, racing to Monk's side.

"You'll have to get used to him," Ham said, jerking his thumb at Monk. "He's part ape. You can never tell how he'll act."

Ignoring this pleasantly, Monk charged for the clearing edge. He hit the brush like a bull moose. He had, he was mortally certain, seen a hand projecting from the brush. A slender, white hand, it was. It looked like a woman's.

The hand had been visible for only a fractional moment, but Monk was certain it had been there. As he searched through the brush, however, he became less positive. There was no sign of any young woman.

Monk studied the ground. As a woodsman, he was no amateur. But in this tangle of rocks and shrubs, not a track could he discover.

Disgusted, he returned to the cabin.

"Don't get excited at what the missing link does," Ham told the attractive Patricia. "Just look at his monkey face, and you'll understand. There couldn't possibly be good sense behind a mug like that."

"Oh, yeah?" Monk grinned. "Listen, you shyster, where has Doc gone to?"

The men glanced about hastily. Monk's words had prepared them for what they found. Doc Savage was not around.

"He's gone!" Patricia gasped. "What on earth can that mean?"

A grin on his homely face, Monk began: "Well, you see, Doc has a habit of——"

"Shut up!" Ham snapped. "I'm doing guard duty here. Go play with your test tubes!"

Monk rambled off, Habeas Corpus at his heels.

There was hardly a mystery about Doc's disappearance. He had simply glided away while the others were watching Monk's wild charge. Once in the brush, he quickened his pace and swung in a wide circle.

Doc had seen the hand which had excited Monk. In fact, the hand had been gesturing at Doc when Monk chanced to glimpse it.

The hand had been feminine, and its owner unquestionably wanted to talk with Doc.

Doc had not gone far when he found a leaf crushed on a rock. A bit farther on, a creeper dangled, torn from its anchorage. There was no breeze here in the undergrowth, yet the creeper swung slowly from side to side. Below it were feminine footprints.

"Señorita Oveja!" Doc called softly.

There was no answer. The swayings of the creeper, however, gradually became shorter and shorter.

"There's no one with me, Miss Oveja," Doc called.

This secured results. Attractive, dark-haired Señorita Oveja appeared in the shrubbery some distance ahead.

"*Buenos dias,*" she greeted. "Good morning. I wanted to talk with you, Señor Savage."

"I recognized your hand," Doc told her.

"Your man—the big, hairy one—frightened me away," Señorita Oveja smiled.

"Monk makes a lot of noise," Doc agreed. "But he wouldn't hurt a fly—unless the fly bit him."

"We have been thinking things over—my father, El Rabanos, and myself," said the girl.

She came closer. Doc noted her olive cheeks were flushed from running.

"You haven't decided you and I may have the same enemies?" Doc asked dryly.

"Then it is that way?" the girl gasped.

"It looks very much like it," Doc admitted. "Our common enemy is a fellow who uses a likeness of a werewolf for his mark."

The beautiful Spanish woman shivered from head to foot. "That is what my father and El Rabanos decided after we talked it over."

"This enemy seems to be after an ivory cube," Doc offered.

Cere started. "You know that, too?"

"Yes," Doc replied. "My cousin, Patricia Savage, has the cube—or did have it."

At this, the Castilian girl showed every evidence of unbounded surprise.

Doc was an expert at reading human character. He was watching her closely. As far as he could tell, her astonishment was genuine. Doc had a suspicion, however, that the man did not live who could read a young woman's mind unfailingly by looking at her pretty face.

"Patricia Savage has it?" gasped Cere.

"Had it," Doc corrected. "The cube seems to have complicated things by disappearing."

"Suppose you tell me——"

"Suppose *you* tell *me*," Doc interposed. "We'll start off with: What gave you the idea that I was your enemy?"

The girl said promptly: "More than a week ago, your uncle, Alex Savage, shot at us from the woods, saying he would kill us unless we left the vicinity."

"Did you see Alex Savage at that time?"

"No. Nor did we see him two days ago when he came again and said that he had sent for you, and that you would come and kill us for not leaving the vicinity."

"Alex Savage warned you again two days ago?"

"Yes."

"It was not Alex Savage!" Doc said flatly.

"But he said his name was Alex Savage!"

"Alex Savage has been dead more than a week."

Cere placed a hand over her heart. "In that case we have been terribly mistaken. This other man was a fake!"

"Any one can be misled," Doc assured her. "Now, suppose you tell me exactly what is behind all this."

The girl nodded. "You have heard of Sir Henry Morgan?"

"The pirate?"

"That is the one," Cere replied. "In the year 1670 he started across the Isthmus of Panama with twelve hundred men. The Spaniards received warning of his coming. Treasure from the Panama City cathedral, and wealth belonging to merchants, was loaded onto a galleon. This craft fled out to sea, carrying some of the owners of the treasure besides the crew."

"That incident is a matter of history," Doc told her. "The pirate Esquemeling, who was with Morgan at the sacking of Panama, wrote of the galleon in his book. Shortly after he had captured Panama, Morgan heard of this treasure craft. He knew the treasure to be of more value than all else the expedition had secured put together. He seized several Spanish boats, and sent them out in pursuit of the galleon. But they did not find the craft."

"And for a very good reason, Señor Savage," Cere resumed. "Part of the galleon crew had mutinied, murdered the merchants and the others aboard, and seized the treasure."

"There is no historical record of such an occurrence!" Doc told her.

"In a moment I'll explain how I know it is true," Cere retorted. "These men who mutinied and seized the galleon loaded with treasure, were not very intelligent. One of them had heard that there was a water passage around North America. He converted his companions to his belief. They sailed north.

"The journey was long and full of hardship. The coast became bleak, and the climate cold. Finally, it was necessary to anchor in a small bay, careen their boat, and make repairs to the hull. They pulled the galleon up on the sandy floor of a small, canyonlike inlet. Bad luck plagued them. An earthquake caused the gulley side to topple over, burying the boat in a sort of cavern."

The Castilian beauty paused to stare steadily at Doc. "The spot where the boat met disaster was only a few miles from here!"

"How do you know that?" Doc demanded.

Señorita Oveja shrugged. "My story will bring that out, Señor Savage. To get back to what happened hundreds of years ago: not all the crew were on the galleon when it was entombed. About a dozen had camped near by. They dug a tunnel to the tomb where their fellows lay. That took many days. Their comrades were dead when reached. No doubt, by now, only their skeletons remain.

"The survivors thought to remove the treasure from the boat, but hostile Indians made that impossible. They determined to leave it and travel southward until they found men of their own race. Later, they would come back by sea.

"One of the men was an expert carver of ivory. He took six small flat pieces of ivory and made a relief carving of the vicinity where the boat lay. He fitted these ivory pieces together, carved portions inward, and made a box. This he packed with clay. Due to the cleverness of his construction, and the clay packing, the box seemed solid."

"The ivory cube!" Doc said understandingly.

"*Si, si!*" Cere assured him. "Even when opened and spread flat, the relief map inside the box would be apparent only to a close observer."

"Go ahead with your story," Doc directed.

"The men closed up the hole which led to the buried ship," Cere resumed. "They started south. Almost at once, they were attacked. Several were slain, including the one who carried the box. The massacre took place under a rock ledge in this vicinity. Those who escaped had to leave the box behind."

The girl made a somewhat shamefaced gesture. "One of those men who escaped was an ancestor of mine. He left a written account of the incident. It was handed down in our family for centuries."

"This clears the situation a lot," Doc told her. "You and your father came for the treasure, eh?"

"Myself, my father, and El Rabanos," Cere corrected. "El Rabanos is financing us."

"You hoped the ivory block would still be under the ledge where the men were massacred?" Doc questioned.

Cere bobbed her attractive head. "Yes. But we were disappointed, señor. It was gone."

"Then you began searching for the galleon itself?"

"*Si, si!* But on this rugged coast, that is a hopeless task."

"And then this fake Alex Savage appeared with his lies, eh?"

"*Si, si!*"

"One thing puzzles me," Doc said.

"Quien sabe?" said the girl. "What is that?"

"How did you happen to be on the train?"

The young woman smiled archly at Doc. Obviously she was captivated by the bronze man's manners and unmistakable character. For the last few minutes she had hardly taken her eyes off him.

Doc realized this, but carefully kept his bronze face expressionless. To Doc, young women were something of a problem. There was no provision in his perilous existence for feminine company. It was necessary for Doc to ignore all eligible girls—for the personal safety of the young things, if for no other reason.

Doc's enemies were legion. They would not hesitate to strike at him through a girl whom they thought he liked.

The prettier the young women were, the harder Doc found it to gently repulse them. The more beautiful the girl, the more stunned she was when the bronze man failed to bow before her charms; and the more vigorous her renewed efforts to ensnare him.

"You have not answered my question," Doc reminded her.

Señorita Cere Oveja colored prettily. "We were on the train to get rid of you, so that you would not give us trouble."

"I trust you didn't contemplate a murder, señorita?" Doc said dryly.

"*Gracias,* no!" the Castilian beauty ejaculated.

Doc Savage nodded slowly. "I can see now why you suspected me," he said. "It was the work of the prowler—the fellow who said he was Alex Savage."

Dark-eyed Cere said eagerly: "He told us he had sent for you to come and take our lives. Naturally, when we got upon the train, we looked upon you as a sort of ogre. We had heard that you were famous for deeds of violence."

"Violence against those who have it coming to them," Doc corrected the pretty señorita.

"My first sight of you brought doubts, Señor Savage," said Cere.

Doc hastily headed her off.

"On the train, some one tried to choke you to death with a leather strap," he said. "Naturally, you thought that was my work."

"*Si, si,*" said Cere. "That is, father and El Rabanos did."

She paused expectantly, as if inviting Doc to ask what her own opinion had been. Doc passed up the opportunity.

"It looked suspicious when you fled the train," he reminded.

"Father and El Rabanos were in terror of you," said the girl. "When the train stopped we decided to flee."

"That brings us down to the present moment, I believe," Doc told her. "Now, what is the purpose of this conversation?"

Cere's entrancing dark eyes dropped.

"Father and El Rabanos are still a little doubtful of you, I regret to say. But they have agreed to talk with you. I wish you would do that."

"You came to persuade me to meet them?"

Señorita Oveja nodded. "*Si, si!* Please do."

"I shall be delighted to accommodate you."

"*Buenos, señor!*" Cere exclaimed. "You make me so happy!"

Doc looked like a fellow who had taken a big swallow of too-hot coffee. He asked: "Shall I go with you now and meet them?"

"Oh, no!" the young woman said hastily. "We are away from our camp now, searching the coast for the buried galleon. You must meet them to-night. Let us say—shortly after sundown. Come alone."

"Alone?" Doc asked sharply.

"Please! If you bring your men, father and El Rabanos will be suspicious of you."

Lifting on tiptoe, Cere pointed through the trees. There was a line of cliffs perhaps a quarter of a mile distant. She seemed to be indicating a gap in these. The opening was like a knife slash.

"Our camp is just beyond that," she smiled. "You can come there?"

"Just through the gap in those cliffs," Doc said. "I'll come —and alone, too."

Usually Doc was an extraordinarily quick mover. There were men who claimed the bronze giant could dodge a bullet. This was a rank exaggeration, of course, but it gave an idea of the speed with which Doc could maneuver himself.

Nevertheless, he now got kissed full on the lips—before he could avoid it. The kiss was clinging, and quite ardent. The Señorita Oveja's lips were entirely delicious, Doc decided.

As if appalled by her act, pretty Cere turned and fled. However, she paused before she was out of sight, and looked back.

Doc Savage had vanished.

Cere turned hastily and went on. She did not head for the gap in the cliff beyond which, according to what she had told Doc, her camp lay. Instead, she angled off to the right.

Unexpectedly, her father and El Rabanos appeared before her.

"We were watching, *hija mío!*" Señor Oveja chuckled. "It was excellently done!"

"As the Americans would say," Cere smiled proudly, "he fell for it—hook, line, and sinker."

"That bronze caballero is no fool," El Rabanos reminded seriously. "Are you sure that he did not suspect he was being tricked?"

"He was like a lamb in my hands," Cere said loftily.

El Rabanos shrugged. "He will be a lion on our hands, if he suspects, señorita."

"What did you tell him?" Señor Oveja demanded.

"As you say, he is clever," the pretty Castilian girl replied. "I did not trust myself to lie to him, so I told the truth. I told him all about our ancestor, and the galleon of treasure from Panama. He claimed to know none of the story."

"He has a tongue tied in the middle—loose at both ends to tell lies!" Señor Oveja snarled. "It was he who made the attempt on the train to kill us."

Cere looked doubtful. "I am not so sure about that, *padre.*"

The father eyed his daughter severely. He made a tongue-clicking sound of disapproval.

"This bronze caballero is very handsome," he said. "A

young woman's opinion of such a man is not to be trusted."

Señorita Oveja stamped her foot. "I knew you would say that! But Señor Savage is not to be harmed!"

"Of course he will not be harmed," El Rabanos put in sharply. "We will merely seize him and hold him as a hostage to insure our securing the ivory cube. We will trade the bronze man for the cube."

"I could slit the big hombre's throat!" Señor Oveja growled.

"There must be no violence!" El Rabanos rapped. "I insist on that."

"Si, si!" the older man mumbled. "As you wish."

They walked off in the direction of their camp.

The camp was nowhere near the cliff, but nearly a mile to the northward. It nestled in a forest of large boulders near a rather rocky stretch of level ground.

At one end of the comparatively level field stood a plane. It was canted over on one wing. A landing wheel was smashed, and the rocks had damaged the wing tip.

El Rabanos stared at the plane and growled in Spanish:

"It is unfortunate that the ship had to hit a rock while I was landing it. We are virtually marooned here in this wilderness."

For shelter, the party had tents. These were small, and of a leaf-green in color.

Cere entered a tent and busied herself improving her appearance. The woods country, she had discovered, was hard on complexions. Moreover, it was difficult for a young woman to be captivating in hobnailed boots, corduroy trousers, and a flannel shirt. This was the garb Cere was wearing, because it was the only raiment which would withstand the rigors of her surroundings.

Señor Oveja and El Rabanos retired to their tents. They were city men, not used to hardship, and each period of exertion called for a corresponding rest.

The woods were quiet. The fog rolled like smoke. It was an altogether dreary day. Faintly, from the distance, came the mushy noise of the waves on the rocky shore line.

Possibly an hour later, in a gloomy stretch of timber something over a mile from the Oveja's camp, a sinister meeting occurred. It was a convention of evil conducted with a furtive caution. It began with the appearance of eleven men. They were swarthy fellows, and they skulked along as if afraid of being seen. Their visages were anything but pleasant to look on.

These were the men who had kidnaped pretty Patricia Savage.

The ominous little caravan of men progressed to a spot where the timber was particularly dense. They clustered together and waited, making no disturbing sound.

"Cere led Doc Savage into the trap for us," a hollow voice said suddenly.

The portentous words were spoken slowly. This, and the fact that the voice was dull and resonant, gave the impression of an exotic drum beating.

Obviously, it was a disguised voice. The speaker was fifty feet or so to the left. He was thoroughly hidden from the group of men by the trees.

The men showed no surprise at the voice. They had been expecting it. Several peered furtively in the direction from which it had come. It was as if they were trying to get a glimpse of the speaker.

"There is no chance of a mistake?" asked one of the men nervously. "This man Savage has an uncanny way of avoiding traps."

The drumlike voice boomed a hollow laugh. "It was a woman who tricked Savage this time. He was too dizzy to suspect anything. You should have seen how still he stood after she kissed him."

"It was clever—using the woman," a man muttered.

"The beauty of it is that she does not know she is being used," said the concealed voice.

A man began sharply: "But I thought that——"

"Oh, the señorita knows she is drawing him into a trap," said the concealed man. "But she does not know that he is to be killed."

"How will we manage it?" questioned one of the group.

"Look off to your right. Do you see that gap in the line of cliffs?"

There was no need of an answer. The rent in the cliffs was plainly distinguishable through an opening in the trees.

"You will post yourselves just inside that opening," said the unseen voice. "You have your machine guns?"

"*Si,*" one fellow muttered, "we have them."

"Set them up just inside the opening in the cliff," their hidden chief ordered. "When Savage appears, you will turn them on him instantly."

"*Si, si.* It will work."

"That is all. Go! *Vamos!*"

Chapter 14

THE TRAP IN A TRAP

The time was approximately one hour before sundown. Doc Savage had not yet informed his men of his meeting with Señorita Oveja. Anyway, of the five, only Monk and Ham were around the cabin.

Monk was absorbed in the kitchen. Test tubes, retorts, mixing bowls, and glass containers of chemicals stood about. Once unpacked, Monk's chemical laboratory seemed of considerable size. Monk was making numberless analysis tests.

So far, he had not announced whether he had drawn any conclusions regarding the weird sleep.

The debonair Ham was having a very enjoyable time entertaining Patricia Savage. The young lady had altogether captivated Ham. Not only was she one of the most beautiful specimens of femininity Ham had ever seen, but she was also one of the most intelligent.

Ham and Patricia were occupying a rustic bench in front of the cabin.

"You wouldn't think it," Ham was saying, "but that homely missing link, Monk, has a wife and thirteen children."

"You don't say!" exclaimed Patricia.

Ham nodded solemnly. "Not only that, but the thirteen children are just like their father. You know—they swing from chandeliers and things."

Patricia looked curiously at Ham. The dapper lawyer's expression was sober as a judge's.

Patricia knew something was amiss. With a face just as straight, homely Monk had told her the same story about Ham. Monk's yarn had differed only in that Ham's thirteen children were half-witted.

"You and Mr. Mayfair are very good friends, aren't you?" Patricia asked.

Ham blinked. He so seldom heard Monk called Mr. Mayfair that he had failed to recognize the name.

"Friends!" Ham exclaimed indignantly. He flourished his sword cane. "Nothing would give me more pleasure than to chop the ears off that missing link!"

The pig, Habeas Corpus, wandered into the vicinity. The shoat sat down and eyed Ham. The pig's actions were strangely human. It raised on its rear legs.

"Who is your trampy-looking pal, Miss Pat?" Monk's ventriloquial voice asked through the medium of the pig's jaws.

Ham launched an indignant kick at the shoat. He might as

well have tried to kick a mosquito. The pig evaded him easily.

Ham glared about in search of the homely chemist. Monk, however, was not in sight. He must have thrown his voice from concealment.

Patricia was laughing heartily. There was something about the easy fearlessness of these men, and the frequent touches of comedy which relieved their doings that was highly satisfying.

Fifteen minutes later, Monk appeared in the cabin door. His homely face was innocent.

"Doc!" he called.

The bronze man appeared from the direction of the boat-house.

"I can't find a thing to indicate what causes the weird sleep," Monk reported.

Numerous times during the afternoon, a plane had prowled overhead. This ship was traveling back and forth systematically. It seemed to be searching for something. It covered the ground twice.

One hunt was made at a very low altitude—less than five hundred feet. The second search was conducted at a greater height—so high that the roar of the motor was barely audible.

Renny was flying the ship, making an aërial photographic map. An uninitiated person would have sworn that no one could take pictures in the fog. But Renny, utilizing infra-rays, was no doubt securing pictures equal to those which could be obtained by sunlight.

For an interval now, however, the plane had not been in evidence.

Not unexpectedly, Renny came out of the brush and strode toward the cabin. The disappearance of the plane from the skies indicated that he had landed some time ago. Under an arm, he carried a bulky package which held camera and photographs.

Entering the cabin, Renny spread his prints on the table. It was not necessary to lose time developing them. The camera was an ingenious type which printed its pictures as they were taken.

"I got a fair layout of the district," Renny reported.

Patricia Savage came in to inspect the work. She was still a bit skeptical about securing pictures in the fog.

"Why!" she ejaculated. "I never saw clearer photographs!"

"Taking pictures with films and lenses sensitive to infra-rays isn't a new idea," Renny told her. "It was a military secret years ago. And for some time it has been utilized on a commercial scale."

"The pictures are in harsh shades," Ham took up the explanation for Patricia's benefit. "Because of that, photography with infra-light is unsuitable for portrait work. A picture taken with infra-light makes you look ugly as sin—like Monk, for instance."

Monk only grinned at the insult.

With a powerful magnifying glass, Doc went to work on the prints. He arranged them in the order in which they had been taken. This gave him an aërial map of the region.

Johnny and Long Tom were still missing. But the bronze man had hardly begun his examination when they appeared.

Johnny removed his spectacles and polished the magnifier on the left side.

"I have little to report," he said. "Of course, I could make only a sketchy inspection of the vicinity. But there was no sign of a valuable ore outcropping. Nor are the rock formations favorable for it."

Doc Savage eyed Long Tom.

"What did you find?" he asked the electrical wizard.

"Nothing particularly unusual about the underlying rock strata," Long Tom said wryly.

"So you guys both drew a blank!" Ham put in.

"Wait a minute!" Long Tom said. "Let me finish. I found something, all right!"

"What?" Doc demanded.

"A rock ledge," Long Tom replied. "With a bunch of skeletons on it."

"That must be where my father found the ivory cube," Patricia offered.

Doc said: "Let's take a look."

Gathering Renny's aërial photographs together, he stuffed them in a pocket.

The ledge was well up on the stony face of a mountain. Too, it was more of an elongated pit dug in a wall of stone, than a ledge. A beetling overhang above made the spot almost a cave. To reach the recess, it was necessary to make a laborious and sometimes dangerous climb.

"Until to-day, my father was probably the only visitor to this spot," Patricia declared.

"I don't wonder," Ham puffed. The climb was wreaking more damage on Ham's clothing.

"This is a swell spot for a goat!" he growled.

The skeletons met their gaze. The bone heaps were white as snow. Cavernous-eyed skulls bore marks hacked by a knife ages ago. These marks explained themselves—the victims had been scalped.

"These are the skeletons of white men," said Johnny, whose knowledge of archæology made his opinion practically indisputable. "They are well preserved, due to the fact that the overhang of the cliffs kept off the weather. This is really a pocket in the side of the mountain."

Doc Savage glanced at Long Tom. "Did you dig up the sand around these bones, then smooth it out again?"

"No," said Long Tom in a startled voice. He peered at the ground.

The sand had been disturbed. All over the ledge it had been dug up and sifted. Then it had been carefully replaced to give the appearance of having been unmolested.

"You were mistaken," Doc told Patricia. "Your father was not the only visitor to this ledge before to-day. From the condition of the sand, it seems a search was made about a week ago."

"They were hunting for the ivory cube!" Patricia gasped.

Doc nodded. "Yes—the cube which remained behind with the massacred galleon crew."

Doc became a magnet for astounded looks.

"Huh!" Monk ejaculated. "You must know something that we don't!"

Doc nodded. Then he told them of his meeting with attractive Señorita Oveja. He repeated, exactly as the girl had told it to him, the story of the treasure galleon from Panama, and the crew who had mutinied. He failed to mention the kiss.

"According to the girl's story," he finished, "the galleon is entombed near here. The relief map inside the ivory cube is the clew to its location."

"But where in blazes is the ivory block?" Monk demanded.

To Monk's query, no answer was forthcoming. Doc Savage, if he had any knowledge on the subject, did not put it into words. The others frankly had not the slightest idea what had become of the troublesome white cube.

Monk peered at the red blur in the fog which marked the position of the sun. It looked like a bonfire on the horizon.

"You say you are to meet the Oveja girl and the two men right after sundown, Doc?"

"Right."

"Then you had better be on your way," Monk said. "It's almost that time."

"Ham, you take Patricia back to the cabin," Doc suggested. "The rest of us had better be, as Monk says, on our way."

For once, Ham looked as if he were not wholly in accord with his job of guarding Patricia. He sensed that he was going to miss some action. Nevertheless, he offered the young lady his arm and guided her away.

"Wait!" Monk called after them. "Miss Pat, would you mind taking Habeas Corpus back with you. The going with us may get kinda tough for the pig."

"Yes, she would!" Ham said indignantly. "She don't want to do it!"

"Why, I'll be glad to," Patricia said contrarily. "I think the pig is very intelligent!"

"Sure he is!" Monk laughed. "Habeas, follow the prettiest girl in the world!"

Habeas Corpus instantly trailed after Patricia and the disgusted Ham.

"The rest of us are going with you, eh?" Monk asked Doc.

"It looks like it."

"But didn't you say you told the girl you would go alone to the meeting place beyond the opening in the cliffs?" Renny put in.

"We're not going to *that* meeting place," Doc replied.

"Huh?" Monk exclaimed.

To explain his change of mind, Doc drew Renny's aërial photographs from his pocket. He spread them on the smooth sand beside the skeletons, then borrowed gaunt Johnny's spectacles. He used the magnifier which was the left lens.

Beckoning his men close, Doc indicated an irregular whitish line on the map.

"There is the line of cliffs," he said. "And there is the opening which the girl told me to walk through. Look close. Notice anything peculiar?"

"Blazes!" Monk exploded. "That opening is the mouth of a blind canyon. There's no sign of a camp in it."

"Look still closer," Doc suggested.

Monk did so, squinting and making grotesque faces. He let out a surprised gasp.

"Look at this!" he told big-fisted Renny, mild voice suddenly fierce.

"Holy cow!" ejaculated Renny after a glance.

"Well, is it a secret?" snapped Long Tom, who had not yet secured a look.

"There's a gob of machine guns planted around that opening in the cliffs," Monk explained. "Men are crouched beside them. The guys didn't bother to get out of sight when they heard Renny's plane. They didn't dream we could take pictures through this fog."

"It's an ambush!" Long Tom snapped.

"Take the head of the class, son," Monk said dryly.

Ignoring him, Long Tom turned to Doc. "Say, did you suspect this before you saw the aërial photographs?"

Doc was slow to answer. "The young woman's insistence that I come alone was slightly suspicious. I'll confess, though, that my doubts were not strong."

"What do we do now?" queried big-fisted Renny. "Go after the guys with the machine guns?"

"We'll call on Señor and Señorita ⤳veja and El Rabanos, first," Doc decided.

"But where *is* their camp?"

Doc indicated the aërial photograph. "It shows on here, and is not very far away. You'll notice the plane they flew here is lying in the clearing beside their camp, apparently wrecked."

A grimly silent, purposeful file, Doc and his men clambered down from the ledge which held the macabre collection of skeletons.

The night had descended with an unexpected abruptness. Surprisingly, with the coming of darkness, the fog had disappeared. Bright stars speckled the sky. A fat, milky bag of a moon leaked its beams.

The night was offering better visibility than the fog-filled day.

An air of expectancy gripped the Señor and Señorita Oveja and El Rabanos, in their camp. They had consumed an evening meal cooked over a gasoline stove which gave forth no smoke.

Pretty Señorita Oveja had cleaned the dishes outdoor fashion, by scouring them with sand, and rinsing them. From the grimaces she made, she apparently did not think much of dish-washing.

"Is it not about time we were going?" she demanded in Spanish.

"*You* are staying here!" her father said calmly.

"But I wish to go!" the young woman retorted.

"No!" the elder Oveja refused firmly.

That settled it as far as Cere was concerned. In her country, young people did not argue with their parents.

"You will not harm the bronze man?" she asked anxiously.

"What happens to Doc Savage is not your affair!" her father snapped. He turned to El Rabanos. "Come, señor, let us be on our way. The meeting time is near."

Señor Oveja went over to get his rifle. It was leaning against a large rock, a rock the size of an automobile.

He reached out for the weapon. Moon shadows darkened the base of the rock like thickly roosting crows.

Señor Oveja suddenly emitted a sound between a whimper and a sob, and fell backward. His body remained perfectly stiff as it tumbled; it retained its rigidity when it hit the sand.

It was as if the señor had turned to stone. The momentum of his fall caused him to rock, like a frame of sticks, from side to side. His arms and legs stuck up with weird stiffness.

"*Padre!*" Cere cried shrilly. "Father!"

Darting forward, the young woman sank beside her parent. She grasped his strangely stiffened arm. The muscles were rigid under her touch. By wrenching, she tried to change the position of one of the arms.

The arm remained at the angle to which she moved it, like the cold limb of a dead man.

"Oh, oh!" wailed Cere. She turned wildly in El Rabanos's direction. She intended to demand his help. But her lips parted and her dark eyes became staring.

El Rabanos had also fallen a victim of the fantastic paralysis. The swarthy, girl-faced man was spread-eagled, as if staked out. His face was turned sidewise, so that moonbeams spilled on it. The features showed no agony—only an unbounded wonder.

"El Rabanos!" Cere cried.

She was close enough to see the man's eyes roll in her direction. It was plain that El Rabanos knew what was going on, but was powerless to move or speak.

What had just happened was the most uncanny occurrence the pretty señorita had ever encountered. She gazed about in terrified bewilderment.

There was not a mark on her father or El Rabanos. There was not a sound from the surrounding shadows to show what had happened.

Suddenly, Cere sought to spring wildly to one side. She moved a trifle too slowly, however.

Bronze hands, floating out of the shadows beside her, trapped her arms. The fingers inclosed like steel bands. The grip, for all of its strength, however, was not tight enough to inflict pain. It was just snug enough to hold the girl tightly.

Cere gave one violent wrench, then realized the futility of that. She relaxed. She knew that Doc Savage must be responsible for the uncanny happening to her father and El Rabanos.

"What have you done to them?" she demanded.

Doc did not answer. Renny and Monk, two mountainous figures, came up in the murk. Johnny and Long Tom approached from the opposite direction.

Doc released Cere. The young woman instantly started to run. She had taken only her second stride when Doc Savage overhauled her, picked her up, and carried her back. His touch was still impersonally gentle, but the Castilian beauty found herself absolutely helpless against his strength.

Cere did not learn what had happened to her father and El Rabanos. The huge forms of Monk and Renny blocked her view as Doc went to the two strangely paralyzed men.

With an experienced sureness, Doc stroked certain nerve centers. Previous pressure on these had induced a sort of paralysis. Doc's practiced touch relieved this condition.

Use of their limbs did not return instantly to the two men; full recovery required perhaps a minute. During that interval, Doc searched Señor Oveja and El Rabanos. Each had a pair of revolvers belted about his middle. Doc removed those. He also took a knife, which he found in a sheath inside Señor Oveja's shirt.

"What does this mean?" Señor Oveja demanded indignantly.

"It means that you weren't as slick as you thought!" rumbled big-fisted Renny.

Oveja glared. "What do you——"

"We have no time for an argument!" Doc interrupted. "Long Tom, Johnny—you guard the prisoners. Monk, you and Renny come with me."

As he spoke, Doc was already gliding away through the moonlight. Renny and Monk pounded after him.

"Where are we headed for?" Monk demanded.

"For that machine-gun ambush at the cliff," Doc told him.

Chapter 15

WHEN TROUBLE DOUBLES

"They're gone!" Monk exclaimed in his small voice.

"Yeah," Renny rumbled. "You can see that they were around recently, too. Here's a match one of them was chewing on. The end is still wet."

Doc and the two men stood on the edge of the blind canyon which penetrated the line of cliffs. They had approached with the greatest of caution. They were sure the ambushers had not seen or heard them. Yet the gang was gone.

Doc Savage listened intently; training had given his ears a keenness which rivaled that of a jungle creature. But they picked up no sound.

"The gang isn't in the vicinity," he decided aloud.

"But how'd they get tipped off?" Renny growled. "How did——"

He shut his thin lips tightly on the rest.

Two loud reports came snapping through the night! They were sharp. Their echoes bounced back and forth with an uproar that sounded like a fantastic dragon coughing!

Monk, confused by the multitude of echoes, demanded: "Where did the shots come from?"

"From the Oveja camp!" Doc decided.

They listened. But a dead stillness had fallen. There were no more shots.

"We'd better go back!" Doc declared.

The bronze man whipped over the brink of the cliff. Below, the drop was almost sheer. Footholds were few and unpleasantly precarious. Yet, Doc seemed to take no particular pains with his going. His speed seemed unaffected by the peril of a fall.

Monk and Renny, tackling the dangerous descent, found it necessary to lower themselves a few inches at a time. Doc was far ahead of them by the time they reached the bottom.

Coming in view of the camp some time later, Monk and Renny received a surprise. They had expected to find violence. However, there was nothing about the scene to indicate anything desperate had occurred.

Señor and Señorita Oveja and El Rabanos stood in the moonlight. Long Tom and Johnny were near. Doc Savage was to one side.

The pig, Habeas Corpus, was galloping slow circles in the moonlight. The shoat's running gait was more than ever like that of a dog.

Monk stared at his pet. "Where did Habeas come from?"

"It came tearing through the brush," Doc explained. "Thinking it was a prowler, Johnny fired a couple of shots in the air. Those were the shots we heard."

"I'm sure Patricia took him back with her," Monk declared. "Ham must have turned him loose. That's the kind of a trick the shyster would pull. He don't think a whole lot of Habeas Corpus."

"I imagine his opinion of the pig is improving a little," Doc declared.

Monk's jaw fell. "What do you mean, Doc?"

By way of answer, Doc Savage produced his tiny lantern, which threw ultra-violet rays. He switched it on, and played the beam on Habeas Corpus.

Letters in an electric blue flame sprang out on the pig's back. Due to the uncertainty of the bristled surface on which they had been drawn, the letters were large and irregular. Each time the pig moved, they seemed to convulse. The letters spelled two words.

SLEEP——GETTING——

"Holy cow!" Renny muttered. "What's that mean?"

"Ham's idea of a joke!" Monk growled.

Doc Savage set out swiftly in the direction of the cabin.

"I hardly think it's a joke," he called grimly. "Long Tom, you stay here and guard these three prisoners."

The electrical wizard nodded, and turned back to watch Señor and Señorita Oveja and El Rabanos.

The other three men ran in Doc's wake toward the cabin.

The cabin was silent as a house of death. It might have been a tomb of logs, erected on the shore of the little inlet. There was no night breeze to flutter leaves in the surrounding brush. Small waves were piling sloppily against the shore. Out on the sea, moonbeams glanced in long silver shafts.

Doc Savage was first to approach the cabin. Renny, Monk, and Johnny brought up the rear. They did not want to spoil any sign with their clumsy tramping.

Using his flashlight, which gave a powerful beam, Doc Savage made a quick inspection of the house. If he had expected signs of violence, he was disappointed. The place was in a no more topsy-turvy condition than it had been when he left.

But there was no sign of Patricia, Ham, or the fat Indian servant.

"It's all right for you fellows to come in!" Doc called, after his first cursory inspection.

Monk lumbered in and looked around. "That's funny! I don't see any signs of a fight. And Ham ain't the kind to give up without a scrap."

Instead of answering this directly, Doc Savage indicated a black smear on the wall of a bedroom. This had the shape of a wolf, with an unpleasantly human face.

"The werewolf!" Monk ejaculated.

"Placed there recently—no doubt by the gang who captured our friends," Doc replied. "The presence of the werewolf mark indicates why there was no struggle."

"How do you figure that?" Monk questioned.

"The strange sleep we have not been able to explain," Doc reminded him. "It seems to strike coincident with the appearance of these werewolf marks."

Doc led the way to the kitchen. Fresh food stood on the table. A sandwich lay on a plate. One bite was missing.

"They must've been having a snack to eat when the thing happened," Renny said.

A saucer, holding a large lump of butter, stood on the table. Doc handed this to Monk.

"Analyze it," he said.

"For crying out loud!" Monk grunted. "What for?"

"Search for the presence of the following chemicals," Doc said, and rattled off a half dozen highly technical laboratory terms.

The chemical terminology was unintelligible to Renny and Johnny. Both were well-educated men, but it was doubtful if either could have picked two comprehensible words out of the list.

Monk nodded with perfect understanding, however. Behind Monk's low forehead, there did not seem room for a teaspoonful of brains. But his looks were deceiving. A roster of the three greatest living chemists would certainly have included Monk.

Taking the platter of butter, Monk went into the room where he kept his portable laboratory. He set to work.

Doc Savage peered closely at the kitchen floor, then took his portable ultra-violet lantern out of his pocket, switched it on, and played the invisible beams on the floor.

A puddle of blue fire seemed to spring into being.

Renny dropped to a knee and rubbed an enormous hand through the glowing spot.

"It's the chalk we use to do invisible writing," he said. "Ham must have dropped his piece. It's been stepped on."

"I think we stepped on it while wandering around in here," Doc said. "My opinion is that Ham, Patricia, and the squaw were in here eating when they felt the weird sleep begin to creep over them. Ham managed to scrawl those words on the pig, Habeas Corpus. He dropped the chalk as he passed out."

Outdoors, a voice hailed loudly.

"Ahoy, the cabin!" it cried. "Don't shoot me!"

Renny and Johnny sprang to a window and looked out. They could see nothing.

Doc's flashlight went out. It made no sound doing so, for the switch was noiseless. The darkness which clamped down was black enough to be solid. Silence lay over the cabin and the surrounding timber. The man who had hailed did not do so again.

"That was Long Tom!" Doc said unexpectedly.

"If it was, his voice was changed!" rumbled big-fisted Renny.

"Something has happened to him, all right," Doc agreed. "But it was his voice."

The bronze man's tone, without seeming to become any louder, suddenly acquired a remarkable carrying quality. It rolled out of the cabin and far away into the brush.

"Come on in, Long Tom!" he said. "What's happened to you?"

There was the sound of shuffling footsteps. Long Tom appeared. The pale-skinned electrical wizard was something of a wreck. He was skinned and bruised, and carried the beginnings of two black eyes.

Long Tom's front teeth were of a large protruding variety. Two of these were missing. The missing teeth had the effect of giving his voice a rather comical, lisping quality. He sounded very much like an irate turkey gobbler.

Monk thrust his head in a door, looked at Long Tom, said: "For cryin' in my sleep! Don't he look funny without them buck teeth!"

"What happened to Señor and Señorita Oveja and El Rabanos," Doc asked Long Tom.

"They took a powder!" gritted the electrical wizard.

"I thought you were guarding them," Renny snorted. A wide grin sat on the big-fisted engineer's usually solemn face. He seemed tickled by the ludicrous appearance which the missing teeth gave the electrical wizard.

"Señor Oveja picked up a rock and whangoed me," Long Tom growled through his missing teeth.

"How'd he catch you off guard?"

The truth, even if it hurt, was the custom of Doc's aides. Long Tom squirmed, felt of the gap where his teeth were missing.

"The darn girl was making eyes at me," he admitted.

Everybody laughed.

"They hit you, then fled?" Doc asked. There was no criticism in his tone.

"Yep," Long Tom admitted. "Señor Oveja followed the rock up with his fists. He walloped me plenty, what I mean! The rock had knocked me too dizzy to dodge."

"Didn't you try to trail 'em?"

"Sure! Kind of a strange thing happened then, Doc. They had not gone far before they managed to get guns. They cut down on me with several shots. I couldn't see 'em. Monkeying around after 'em was useless, with me disarmed."

"Guns!" Renny ejaculated. "But we took their guns when we seized them in their camp."

"Yeah. They must have had other weapons hidden in the brush."

Doc said: "Monk, how about analyzing that butter?"

Monk nodded and returned to his work over the portable chemical laboratory. He had spread his paraphernalia over a large table. Several of the mixing trays were giving off strong-smelling odors.

Going outdoors, Doc searched for tracks. Finding them was a simple matter for his trained eye. In addition to the tracks of Patricia, Ham, and the squaw, there were prints of at least half a dozen other men. The trail did not wander, but headed for the shore.

The procession of footprints crossed a spot where the ground was soft. Doc got down on all fours to make an examination; then he stood up.

"The same gang that we rescued Pat from has seized her again," he said. "I've seen some of those footprints so often they're beginning to look like the tracks of old friends."

The trail terminated near the boathouse. Certain marks in the soft sand might have been made by canoe keels. Doc looked into the boathouse. The canoes which had been stored there were missing.

"They came by land," he said. "But they left by water. That was a wise trick on their part. We haven't a chance of trailing them over water."

At this point, Monk came running from the direction of the cabin. He was excited. He had never looked more like a gorilla than now.

The pig, Habeas Corpus, bounded at his heels, making frantic efforts to keep up.

"I've got it!" Monk shouted. "I've got it!"

"Got what?" Doc demanded.

"The stuff in the butter!" Monk bawled. "You know how butter absorbs the odor of any smelly food you put in the refrigerator with it? Well, when the house was saturated with this stuff, the butter absorbed enough of it for me to find it by making an analysis."

"Listen, you homely missing link!" Renny rumbled. "What have you found?"

"The stuff which caused the mysterious sleep," Monk grinned. "It's an odorless and colorless gas which is poisonous if inhaled long enough."

Renny, Long Tom, and Johnny were plenty surprised at this development. Doc Savage, however, had expected it. He had already surmised the probable cause of the weird slumber. So closely had he guessed that he had told Monk what chemical components to look for.

"No doubt the stuff was used to kill Alex Savage," Monk said. "To a physician who did not have much experience, and who did not suspect foul play, the effects of the stuff might look like heart failure."

Long Tom grimaced, felt of the gap in his teeth. "I didn't think the stuff was poisonous. You know it didn't kill us on the train."

"That was because you didn't get enough of it," Doc replied. "I thought at first that the attack on the train was made merely to frighten us. Since then, I've learned more of the nature of these fellows. They would as soon kill us as try to scare us.

"Just why such a small quantity of gas was injected into our train compartment is hard to explain. Perhaps the fellow administering the gas was frightened away. The stuff must have been sent into the compartment through the crack at the bottom of the door."

Doc ended his long speech abruptly, and cupped a palm back of an ear. He stood thus for several seconds, perfectly rigid.

"There's a boat coming!" he said. "It sounds like an outboard engine."

A minute passed—two—three. The others began to wonder if Doc could have been mistaken. Then they heard the sound of the boat.

"Probably the kidnapers coming back to make a deal!" Renny boomed.

"The boat is coming straight in from the open sea," Doc decided.

The boat nosed in past the floating mail box. It became distinguishable in the moonlight. It was simply a square-sterned canoe, fitted with an outboard motor.

"Ahoy, señors!" called a hoarse voice.

"I've got a notion to take a shot at him!" Renny rumbled. "Bet I can hit him!"

"And then they'd bump Ham, Patricia, and the squaw!" Monk grunted. "Don't be a dope!"

Monk was very earnest. Although Monk and Ham seemed continually on the point of flying at each other's throats, and insulted each other with vigor and delight, either would have risked his life for the other. On occasion, each had done so.

"What do you want?" Doc called to the distant men.

"The ivory block, Señor Savage!" the fellow shouted back.

"We haven't got the block!" Doc told him.

"You cannot deceive us, hombre!" the reply came volleying back. "The Señorita Savage had it. She admitted that fact when she was our prisoner earlier."

"She *thought* she had it," Doc corrected him. "When she looked in the hiding place, the block was gone."

"We are not interested in hearing a smooth story, Señor Savage," said the distant man. "I came to inform you of a fact."

"What fact?"

"Simply, señor, that we now have your six friends in a very safe place."

Several seconds of surprised silence followed these words.

"Six!" Renny's big voice rumbled.

"Ham, Patricia, and the squaw—that's only three!" muttered Johnny. He took off his glasses with the magnifying lens, fingered them thoughtfully.

"Did you say six?" Doc called to the boatman.

"Si, si," the fellow shouted back.

"He can only mean one thing," Long Tom said slowly. "I told you that the Ovejas and El Rabanos started shooting at me right after they escaped."

"You were evidently mistaken," Doc told him.

"Sure I was!" Long Tom agreed. "It was this other gang shooting at me. They must have grabbed Señor and Señorita Oveja and El Rabanos."

Renny banged his big fists together. "It beats me!"

"Me, too," Monk agreed. Bewilderment was on his homely face. "I figured Señor Oveja, his daughter, and El Rabanos were in with the other gang. The ambush they fixed for Doc made me think that."

"I figured the same way," said Johnny. "There must have been a contact between the two parties. Otherwise, how did they know of the meeting with Doc?"

"The girl and the two men might have set a snare to capture me," Doc pointed out. "The other gang, hearing of it, could have tried to turn it into a death trap."

"That might be, too," Johnny admitted.

The man in the distant boat had been waiting. His boat had drifted near a large rock which thrust out of the bay; he had wedged the end of a boat hook into a crack in this rock, and was holding his little craft stationary. The rock was a bullet-proof shelter.

"Do you understand me, señor?" the man yelled. "I have your six friends! They are all safe—so far!"

"Ham, Patricia, and the squaw!" Doc called. "Who are the other three?"

"El Rabanos, Señor Oveja, and his daughter!" came the reply.

"I told you so!" said Long Tom. "When the three got away from me, they jumped from the fryin' pan to the fire. That explains why the machine gunners weren't at the cliff when you arrived. They were watching the Ovejas' camp, and saw us show up there. Then they skipped."

"This seems to indicate the señorita is straight, after all," Monk grunted.

"When she said they were camped behind the cliff, she lied," Johnny reminded him.

"You want to make a swap?" Doc shouted.

"Si, si, señor!" the man in the canoe called hastily. "We will trade our prisoners for the ivory cube."

"I told you we haven't got the ivory cube!" Doc called back.

"You are lying, señor," called the canoeman. "I will return in two hours. If you do not give me the ivory cube, one of the prisoners will be shot, and the body tossed out where it will drift ashore!"

With that, he started the outboard motor, and the square-stern canoe skipped out to sea. Apparently, he had laid down an ultimatum about which there could be no argument.

Chapter 16

INSIDE THE IVORY BLOCK

The boat had hardly started its seaward retreat when Doc Savage whirled on Long Tom.

"Your electrical ear!" he said. "Get it!"

Long Tom dashed for the cabin.

Just as Monk always carried chemical equipment, so did Long Tom carry a variety of electrical devices. Among these was an apparatus which had been useful on many occasions. This consisted of a compact, highly sensitive parabolic microphone pick-up, together with an amplifier of great power. The thing was no radical departure from the listening devices military men use to spot enemy airplanes. However, it was infinitely more compact.

Long Tom hurriedly assembled the mechanism. The microphone was directional. He pointed it at the receding motor canoe. The outboard engine was no longer audible to the unaided ear.

Long Tom twisted the dial on his amplifier. There was a loud-speaker device. The sound of the retreating canoe poured out with loud volume.

They listened to the noise which the sensitive device picked up. After a while the outboard died suddenly.

Long Tom turned the amplifier on full force. A mosquito flew across the front of the microphone, and sounded like a trimotored airplane. Then the listener picked up several faint shouts, but they were not understandable.

"Holy cow!" Renny thumped. "They must be holding the prisoners in a boat out at sea!"

"Take flashlights," Doc directed suddenly. "And hunt for birds' nests in pine trees."

"Huh?" Monk grunted, and looked as if he had not understood.

"Birds' nests in pine trees," Doc repeated. "We're not interested in birds' nests in any other kind of trees, though."

"What do we do when we find them?" Monk wanted to know. He was still puzzled.

"Climb up and look in them," Doc said.

"Then what?"

"When you find the right bird's nest, you won't need to be told."

The four men went looking for birds' nests. Each had a dubious and puzzled look on his face. Just why Doc was abruptly interested in nests in pine trees, they had no idea.

Monk cast his light up a tree and spied a telltale knot of twigs, stringy bark, and feathers. He prepared to shin up to the nest.

"Huntin' birds' nests!" he snorted. "I'm glad Ham ain't here to see! Would he hand out razzberries!"

"I wouldn't blame him!" Renny boomed. "Especially since you're looking for nests in pine trees."

"Pine trees—sure!"

"That's a spruce you're starting to climb!" Renny chuckled.

"Yeah, it is at that," Monk admitted sheepishly, after taking a second look.

Doc Savage returned to the cabin. He switched on his flashlight, which gave the brilliant beam. From a pocket he drew the aërial photographs which Renny had made. As yet, Doc had not had time to make a complete examination of these photographic prints. He did so now.

On a picture which had been taken something like seven miles up the coast, he found a tiny grayish spot. This might have been a faded, elongated flyspeck. But under a magnifying glass, it became a small schooner.

A tender dangled on a painter behind the schooner—a canoe, fitted with an outboard.

The discovery convinced Doc that it was upon this boat that the prisoners were being held.

The craft was now standing out to sea, of course.

Monk came plunging in from the night.

"I found it, Doc!" he howled.

The gorillalike giant of a chemist held his prize in both hands. It was a bird's nest—the nest of a very large bird, judging from its size.

"How did you know what to look for, Doc?" Monk questioned.

"Remember the amber-colored, sticky stuff we found on the trousers and on the hands of the murdered Indian?" Doc asked.

"Sure!"

"It was gum off a pine tree."

Monk whistled softly, comprehending. "There was some bark stuck to his trousers, and tiny feathers stuck to his hands."

"Bark off a pine tree and feathers from a bird's nest," Doc agreed.

Monk dived a furry hand into the bird's nest.

"Hocus pocus presto!" he grinned.

He brought out a block of ivory more than two inches square.

Renny and Johnny and Long Tom came in. They stared at the block.

"Boat Face stole it!" Renny thundered. "That's where it went! He hid it in a bird's nest!"

Doc took the block and turned it in his hand. The workmanship was wonderful. The thing looked perfectly solid.

Crooking a finger at Monk, Doc said: "I've got a job for you."

The bronze giant and the homely chemist retired to the room which held Monk's portable laboratory. Two or three minutes elapsed. When Doc reappeared, he was alone. He carried the block in one hand.

On a foundation of books, Doc arranged two flashlights so that they splashed a brilliant glare on the table. He placed the ivory cube in the illumination.

Johnny promptly handed over his glasses with the magnifying left lens. The magnifier disclosed narrow, straight cracks along all four corners of the ivory block. They were too small for the eyes to see unaided.

With his powerful hands, Doc tested the construction of the cube. He was uncertain just how it opened. He tried gentle pressure, without result. He shook it violently, much as one would shake the mercury down in a thermometer. This caused the block to separate into six sections. It had been held together by tiny, ingenious dowel pins.

The core of the cube was a hard, square block of dried mud. Doc inspected this curiously. He turned the mud slowly in his palm. Then, wheeling abruptly, he went into another room.

Boat Face had been buried. His squaw, however, had kept the clothing he had been wearing at the time of his death. Doc selected the trousers and turned the pockets inside out. He had done this on a previous search, but he wanted to make sure.

Several flat leaves, fragments of chewing tobacco, came to light. The tobacco was very black in color.

Doc turned his attention to the mud cube which he had crushed in his palm. There was a leaf of the black tobacco in the mud. Boat Face's chewing tobacco inside the cube!

From Monk's room came brisk tinkling of test tubes and mixing beakers.

Doc's other three aides had been watching the bronze man. Their expressions showed plainly that they were going to ask questions.

But before they could interrogate him, they all heard the mutter of an approaching outboard motor.

Doc Savage whipped outdoors. Three of his men followed him. Monk, however, stayed with the job he was doing.

The sputter of the outboard loudened. A blurred spot appeared out to sea. It soon resolved into the square-sterned canoe. The speedy little craft was crowded with men.

In the gloom, little could be seen of the canoe passengers. Their forms were dark humps. From each hump a slender, black thorn seemed to project. This proved they were not the prisoners—the thorns were rifle barrels.

The outboard stopped, and the canoe coasted behind a rock. The armed passengers used boat hooks to keep themselves sheltered behind the stony hump. One or two could be seen using binoculars. They discerned Doc Savage and his aides.

"Your decision, Señor Savage!" one shouted.

"We have found the block," Doc told him.

"You had it all the time!" the man jeered.

Doc did not argue. "Where are the prisoners?" he called.

"They will be produced when you are ready to make the trade."

"I'm ready now."

The men in the motor canoe held a brief consultation. One of the gun barrels was pointed upward. There was a loud report. Evidently the weapon was a shotgun.

Nothing happened for three or four seconds. Then, high overhead, there was another report and a blinding flash.

"Regular Fourth of July!" said Renny.

"It was a flash rocket, fired as a signal," announced Johnny.

"The prisoners will soon be here," called the man from the outboard canoe.

Nothing more happened for possibly fifteen minutes. Then, far out to sea, the slow throb of a marine engine came into hearing.

Doc listened intently to the engine noise.

"It's a gasoline motor," he decided. "That means there is probably an auxiliary power plant in the schooner."

Shortly afterward, using glasses, Doc was able to discern the craft. It was not more than fifty feet long, but had a wide beam and stout lines. The boat was built for service.

Outside the inlet, it swung into the teeth of a light breeze. The auxiliary motor, turning slowly, held it stationary.

"The prisoners are aboard the schooner, señor!" called the man in the motor canoe.

"How do you know that?" Doc countered.

Shouts passed between the canoe and the schooner. Following this, Ham's voice rang strongly from the schooner. Ham had a powerful orators' voice, developed by much courtroom work.

"We're all O. K.!" he shouted. "If they're trying to bargain for our release, Doc, tell 'em to go take a jump at the moon!"

"Are there six of you?" Doc demanded.

"Sure! Señor and Señorita Oveja, and El Rabanos, are prisoners, too!"

Then the spokesman in the canoe interrupted the conversation.

"Will you turn over the ivory cube for their release?" he called to Doc.

Doc lowered his voice so that it could by no chance reach any of the swarthy men.

"Monk!"

"Coming up!" said Monk, also low-voiced.

The homely chemist ambled out of the cabin. His hairy

hands swung well below his knees. One paw gripped an object wrapped in a handkerchief.

"All set?" Doc asked.

"Yep. But I was sure pushed for time."

Doc and Monk strode together down to the water's edge. For a moment, they were lost to view in the moonlight as they worked through the brush. They waded out until the lapping waves came somewhat above their knees.

"Come and get it!" Doc called. "But you must release the prisoners!"

"Si, si!" called the man in the canoe. "The captives will be turned loose the instant we have the ivory block."

The outboard motor bawled; its propeller threw up a fan of spray. The canoe darted inshore with the speed of a frightened duck.

At a low word from Doc, Monk retreated hastily and got under cover.

The canoe swerved inshore and slackened speed. The boat passed Doc slowly at a distance of thirty feet.

"Throw the cube!" commanded a man. "It had better fall in the canoe, too! We dare not come too close to you. We will free the prisoners when we have it!"

Doc's arm drew back, shot forward. Square and white, the little block sailed through the moonlight. The man in the canoe caught it.

"Bueno!" he barked. "Good! Now—this is how we intend to return the prisoners."

As if the exclamation were a signal, every man in the canoe lifted his rifle. The muzzles lipped flame. Gun sounds blended in a ragged roar!

At the moment when he tossed the white cube, Doc Savage was standing in water above his knees. He was not taken unawares. The first rifle barrel was hardly swaying toward him when he doubled, flopping forward violently into the water. He was completely submerged before the shots crashed.

The perfect physical condition in which Doc kept himself had given him an ability which had saved his life on other occasions. This was the capacity to hold his breath for a seemingly impossible interval!

Actually, the breath-holding did not depend entirely on physical condition. There was a trick to it. Instead of taking as deep a breath as he could, several rapid inhalations were made to charge the lungs with oxygen, and the dive was then made with a normal amount of air in the lungs. Doc had learned this trick from the men who could do it best—South Sea pearl divers.

Keeping close to the sandy bottom, Doc swam under water. He did not go toward the canoe. Nor did he swim fast enough to raise a betraying ripple.

The water was vibrant with hollow *chunging* noises— rifle shots. The men were driving lead at random, in hopes of making a hit.

As he swam, Doc's hands encountered a rock. He eased around it, still submerged. When the rock was between himself and the canoe, he floated to the surface.

He was in time to hear the first of a series of remarkable sounds.

These noises resembled the moan of a gigantic bull fiddle. They were so loud they hurt the ears. The moans were very short, none lasting more than two seconds. The cove throbbed with their volume.

These sounds were strings of shots, although a human ear could not distinguish between the reports. They came so swiftly as to seem a single shot. The shots were fired by the remarkably compact little machine guns which were Doc's invention.

Doc chanced to look. Being in shadow, he was fairly safe from discovery. The little machine guns were charged with bullets which carried unconsciousness rather than death— mercy bullets.

Three men were down in the canoe. This was not such good shooting, considering that all of Doc's men were good marksmen. Rather, it was evident, they were not trying to capture the gang.

The canoe turned wildly and skittered out toward the bay mouth. A few bullets followed it, fighting wave crests like angry bees. It was noticeable that none of the slugs came close to the canoe, which was now in wild flight.

"It is bad shooting, and this is lucky for us!" squawked a man.

"Those guns!" shivered another. "Never before have I heard anything like them, señors!"

The terrific rate at which the little machine guns fired had produced a near terror. They all showed the effects of it.

The three men who had been hit lay motionless in the bottom of the canoe. As soon as the ugly moans of the machine guns ceased, the three victims were examined.

"*Bueno!*" ejaculated one of the gang. "They are not dead!"

Continuing his inspection, the man gave a grunt of surprise.

"What is this? The bullets seem to have penetrated only skin deep, and then burst!"

Evidently the man had never seen a mercy bullet. He and

his fellows were puzzling over the slugs when the canoe reached the schooner. They clambered aboard, after lifting their three motionless companions over the rail.

"Did you get the ivory block?" asked a fellow who seemed to be in charge of the boat.

"We did!" declared one of the group. He pulled the white cube from a pocket, and passed it over.

The other examined it.

From the shore, a strange sound drifted. It was a series of guttural, booming words—words which were intelligible to no one on the schooner deck.

It was Doc Savage, shouting in a strange dialect.

The man holding the white block looked at his fellows. "Do any of you understand that language, amigos?" he asked.

There was a general shaking of heads. The tongue in which the shout had been couched was wholly foreign to anything they had ever heard.

Dismissing the shout as unimportant, the men examined the white cube closely. They sought to get it open. Finally, they shook the cube violently. It separated into six sections.

What happened then was strange. The holder of the cube stared stupidly at the segments. Then he leaned over and gazed foolishly down at the deck. And, as if he had found a place to lie down, he toppled forward.

His fall upon the deck produced a loud thump. He lay quite motionless afterward.

Chapter 17

INTO THE EARTH

The apparent magic which had felled the opener of the box reached swiftly to the other members of the crew. One went down. Another! There was no outcry, no attempt to flee. They simply keeled over.

Each man began snoring softly a few seconds after he had sprawled out.

After perhaps twenty seconds, not a man on the schooner's deck remained upright.

Ham and the other prisoners were below. They had been locked in a small, not too clean cabin. The wrists of each were bound tightly. A long rope had been knotted to the lashings of Ham's wrist, carried to those of pretty Señorita Oveja, and tied, thence to the señorita's father, and the rest of the prisoners.

While men were dropping so mysteriously on deck, the prisoners were doing something that seemed inexplicable.

They were holding their breaths. Señor Oveja's cheeks were puffed with the effort. He seemed about to explode.

With one hand, Ham made slow counting gestures, as if he were measuring the passage of a certain length of time.

Finally, Ham let his breath out in a rush and said: "O. K.! You can start breathing again."

"What was the idea of telling us to hold our breaths, Ham?" Patricia Savage questioned curiously.

"Did you hear Doc shout in that strange language?" Ham asked.

"Yes. I couldn't understand a word of it."

"Probably not a dozen people in the so-called civilized world could understand it," Ham told her. "The language was ancient Mayan. Doc and the rest of us speak it and understand it."

"What did Doc say when he shouted?"

"He said he had some of his anæsthetic gas in the ivory cube," Ham replied. "He said for us to hold our breaths, because the stuff would be released when the cube was opened."

"But why hold our breath?" Patricia queried, puzzled.

"The anæsthetic gas spreads with lightning swiftness," Ham explained. "In less than a minute it dissolves and becomes ineffective. We simply held our breaths until it was dissipated."

Ham now got to his feet. His ankles were not bound, so this was comparatively simple. The others followed his example. Ham headed for the deck. The others had no choice but to follow him. They were tied in a chain by the rope.

Patricia gasped in surprise when she saw the sleeping forms of her late captors.

"The gas got them!" Ham chuckled. "Now, if we can just get this boat headed for shore, we'll be all right."

"Did it work?" Doc called loudly from the beach.

"You tell 'em!" Ham bellowed back. "Like a charm!"

"The engine of the launch won't run," Doc called. "There's no gasoline in the tank. But we'll paddle out and help you get to shore."

"You want to be careful!" Ham called. "The whole gang wasn't on the boat. We've only got about half of them."

"Any idea where the others are?" Doc shouted.

"No!" Ham said. "They're liable to be around somewhere."

Doc made no answer.

Ham, unable to distinguish the bronze man in the moonlight, decided Doc had gone to get the launch.

Patricia glanced uneasily at the swarthy men lying senseless on deck.

"Aren't you afraid they'll revive?" she asked Ham.

"It will take them nearly two hours to wake up," Ham told her. "Doc has been using this anæsthetic gas for a long time. I know exactly how it functions."

Patricia heaved a relieved sigh. "Then we're safe!"

She was too optimistic.

Unexpectedly, from either side of the schooner, rifles banged! The shots echoed back noisily from the cliffs. Bullets chopped savagely at hull and deck house. A slug tore a ragged hole in the furled sail.

The men doing the shooting were as yet some distance away. Ham, peering hard, could locate them only from the flash of their rifles. They were coming from two directions. Evidently they were shooting at the schooner as a whole; at that distance they could not pick out individual targets.

"It's the rest of the gang!" Ham gritted.

El Rabanos wailed: *"Diablos!* The devils! They will kill us!"

"Get in the canoe," Ham commanded. "Let me in the stern, where I can start the motor."

Patricia cried: "But the schooner was——"

"No time to get it under way," explained Ham. "Come on, those birds must've been listening. They heard us talking to Doc, and knew something had happened to their pals."

Privately, Ham had no use for canoes. Years ago, one had ducked him when he was togged out in his immaculate clothes. They were tricky things, even when there was plenty of time to get into them.

Getting six excited individuals, all linked together by a rope, into the canoe, proved to be an agonizing job. Twice the canoe rocked sickeningly. Ham groaned and yelled by turns.

The instant he could reach the outboard motor at the stern, he went to work on it. The motor was still hot. That was lucky, for, with his hands bound, he would never have got it started otherwise.

Rifle bullets were still hitting the schooner with loud *chugs!* Some bit at the water and ricocheted with piercing wails! Others traveled on without touching water or schooner, and *spanged* noisily among the rocks on the inlet shores.

The outboard motor popped a blue flame through its exhaust ports. It fired again, then began to moan regularly.

Patricia, in the bow, had already thrown off the painter. Ham gave the outboard all the gas it would take. The canoe swerved away from the schooner.

A spatter of lead followed them as they raced for shore. The riflemen, approaching from two directions, were not yet close enough to shoot accurately, however.

A bullet *spanged* through the thin canvas side of the canoe, just at the water line. The hole, near the bow, began to let water in.

"I hope lightning doesn't strike twice in the same place," Patricia said, and put a hand over the bullet hole to shut out the water.

It was the little supermachine guns in the hands of Doc and the others which insured their reaching shore. The small guns began to emit the amazing bull-fiddle moans.

The bullets, charged with tracer chemical in addition to the sleep-producing potion, raced like red-hot wires through the moonlight. It was probably the sight of the red cords of tracer snapping past their faces that moved the riflemen to stop shooting. Whatever the cause, they fell silent.

Ham ran the canoe against the beach so hard that it skidded up half its length on the sand. He piled out, dragging the others.

The giant form of Doc Savage materialized silently beside them. Doc produced a knife and cut through their bonds.

"Your scheme was swell!" Patricia told Doc.

"Give Monk the credit," Doc replied. "He is the one who made up that fake ivory block. He's a wizard as a chemist, or he couldn't have done it so quickly."

Ham overheard this, and he grimaced. Praise for the homely Monk was a pain to his ears.

The tall, girl-faced El Rabanos came up.

"I wish to apologize for any trouble I may have caused you, Mr. Savage," he said earnestly. "I know now that you are not our enemy."

Señor Oveja approached in time to listen. He emitted a surly growl.

"*En verdad!*" he snapped. "Indeed! I am by no means convinced that Savage is our friend."

Big, bronze Doc Savage did not seem particularly interested in what Señor Oveja thought. He turned away.

Girl-faced El Rabanos said in a low voice:

"I am terribly sorry for my friend's actions, Señor Savage."

"Don't worry about it," Doc said wryly.

"But, Señor Savage, it is ungrateful of him, I am sorry to say," El Rabanos insisted. "Those hombres on the schooner were going to kill us! Unquestionably you saved our lives."

Doc said nothing. He kept on walking; he was headed for the cabin.

"We owe you an explanation also," El Rabanos continued in an ingratiating voice. "In case you do not know it, we prevailed upon the Señorita Oveja to deceive you this afternoon."

"I knew it."

"We did not intend to harm you with the trick," El Rabanos said desperately. "We were merely going to seize you. We had the silly idea that we could trade you to your friends for the ivory cube. We had finally decided you must have the cube, but did not know its significance."

Pretty Señorita Oveja overhauled them and joined in the conversation.

"That is the truth, Señor Savage," she added her insistence. "Harm to you was the last thing in our minds."

Doc bowed politely, but said nothing.

A few minutes later, however, when Doc and Monk were together, the homely chemist expressed a private idea.

"Doc," said Monk, "I may be wrong, but I believe there's a connection between our three visitors and that gang out there."

"What makes you think so?"

"The fact that the trap set for you was a death trap."

Doc's strange flake-gold eyes rested intently on the homely chemist. "Who do you suspect, Monk?"

Monk tugged slowly at an ear which resembled a gristle tuft.

"Señor Oveja," he said.

Doc Savage did not change expression. Neither did he speak further on the subject. Instead, he spread a piece of paper on the table, then he drew an envelope from a pocket, and tore off the corner. From envelope to paper, he poured a tiny heap of clean white sand.

"Where'd that sand come from?" Monk queried curiously.

"From the moccasins of the dead Boat Face," Doc told him. "Guess you were not around when I took it out."

Going to the door, Doc called: "Pat!"

Patricia, alert, and prettier than ever, entered. She gave Monk a gorgeous smile, apparently by way of thanking him for his work in constructing the trick ivory block which had been responsible for their escape.

Monk reacted with the look of a homely cat which had just dined on the canary.

Patricia was by far the prettiest girl Monk had ever seen. He would have liked to stay and talk with her. A glance at Doc, however, showed that the bronze man wanted to be left alone with Patricia.

Monk ambled out, leaving the two together.

Hardly more than a minute later, Patricia reappeared. She looked neither to right nor left, but walked away, along the shore of the inlet.

She was swallowed by the black shadows which gorged the wilderness of brush.

Doc Savage came out of the cabin and moved about in the darkness until he found Long Tom.

"Take your listening device and climb up on top of the cabin," Doc directed the electrical wizard. "Swing the thing in slow circles. Report whatever you hear."

Long Tom hastily complied. The microphone of his contrivance was so sensitive, and the amplifier so powerful, that it would be almost impossible for any one to approach the cabin without being heard. Long Tom hooked wires together, clicked switches, and thumbed dials. Instead of a loud-speaker for listening, he used a head set. This was more sensitive.

"Hey, Doc!" he called almost at once. "I hear somebody already. It sounds like one person walking."

"Is the person making three sharp rapping sounds at frequent intervals?" Doc asked. "Sounds such as would be made by sticks beaten together?"

Long Tom strained his ears. "Yes."

"Then it's Patricia," Doc told him. "I gave her two pieces of wood, and told her to beat them together three times every few steps. Whenever you hear that, you'll know it's her. If you hear anybody else, though, fire two shots in the air. That's to warn Patricia to hide herself, or to hurry back."

"What's Patricia doing?" Long Tom asked.

There was no answer from the bronze man. Long Tom looked over the cabin roof. He could see no sign of Doc in the moonlight. He returned to his listening, deciding Patricia's mission would have to be a mystery for the present.

Doc had entered the cabin. On a table, he spread the six sections which had been fitted together to form the ivory block. At first glance, the inner surfaces of these seemed merely carelessly carved. They were a bit rough. However, when a magnifying glass was put on them, the roughness assumed a definite form. It was possible to tell that the block held a cleverly carved relief map of the region around the cabin.

It was necessary to rearrange the parts several times before Doc had them in their proper positions.

"That's it!" Renny said at last. Renny was looking over Doc's shoulder. The big-fisted fellow probably knew as much about maps as any man. It was part of his engineering training.

Doc ran the magnifying glass along the irregular line which indicated the shore on the carving. It was not hard to find the location of the entombed galleon.

The spot was marked by a tiny, exquisitely carved skull. There was no other peculiar mark on the map, which made it almost certain the skull identified the location of the galleon.

"The darn thing isn't over a mile from here!" Renny boomed.

Señora Oveja, his daughter, and El Rabanos had not been parties to the inspection of the insides of the ivory block. Chancing to come into the room now, they observed what had been going on.

"I demand that block!" Señor Oveja said angrily. "It is mine!"

"By what right?" Doc queried.

Señor Oveja sputtered indignantly. "My ancestor——"

"Your ancestor was a thief," Doc said shortly. "The ivory block was admittedly not his property. Nor was the galleon or its contents."

Señor Oveja seemed about to explode. Before he could do that, Doc walked away. The bronze man had the sections of the ivory block in a pocket.

"You fellows drift out in the brush," Doc told Monk in a low voice. "I'll join you a bit later. It'll save trouble with Señor and Señorita Oveja and El Rabanos, if they do not know we are going. We'll leave Long Tom here to watch them. Long Tom has to stay anyway, to protect Patricia with his listening device. He has to give Pat warning if any of our enemies come close, so she can duck."

"We're going to have a look at that galleon?" Monk guessed in a hushed whisper.

"You have guessed it," Doc told him.

Twenty minutes later, Ham was hissing peevishly at Monk, "Can't you be quiet, you missing link! You make more fuss than all the rest of us together!"

This was hardly true. Ham had just fallen down, making a considerable racket.

Monk only sniffed. "Why don't you throw that sword cane away, shyster? That's what you're stumbling over."

The dapper Ham had retained his sword cane through the excitement. He had lost it in the cabin when the gang seized him. Upon escaping, his first act had been to find it.

"You tripped me!" Ham growled. "You big accident of nature——"

"Cut out the funnyboning, you culls!" Renny's big voice boomed softly. "The dog-gone galleon should be around here some place!"

The sloppy smack of waves began to reach their ears. Each smack was followed by a long flutter of falling spray. This indicated the shore was a rock wall climbing sheer from the water.

Like mountaineers, the men were carrying a long rope. This was vitally necessary. The way they were traversing was incredibly rough. Deep gashes appeared underfoot with the unexpectedness of crevasses in a glacier.

More than once, they had to lower a man over a lip of stone until he touched bottom. Just as often, they had to remain at the foot of a wall of stone while Doc Savage climbed with the end of the rope, later to haul them up. To Doc's enormous strength, agility, and sense of balance, the canyon walls presented no great obstacles.

Eventually, Doc's men sank on the crest of a small ridge, panting. They rested there. Doc had gone on ahead while they climbed. They presumed he was searching for the spot marked on the map within the ivory cube.

"Here it is, men!" Doc called suddenly.

The men came to life as if lightning had struck near by. They scrambled down the steep slope toward the spot Doc's voice had come from.

The bronze man stood beside a waist-high pile of evergreen brush. The spot was in a cuplike depression. On all sides, stone walls sloped up steeply.

The gaunt Johnny looked around vacantly. He took off his glasses, put them back on again.

"I don't see anything," he said.

Doc Savage grasped a limb which projected near the bottom of the brush pile. He lifted it, and upset the entire pile.

The brush had covered a hole in the steep slope of the hill—the mouth of a tunnel. It was perhaps three feet wide, four high.

For a few feet, the tunnel penetrated soft earth. For that

distance, it was timbered. The timbers were bright and new. In some spots, twigs still clung to them. Leaves on these were still green.

Beyond the timbering, the tunnel dived into solid rock and sloped sharply downward. Its floor became a series of crude steps.

"This work was done a long, long time ago," said Johnny. If any one was qualified to judge the age of mankind's handiwork, the gaunt archæologist was. He could look at a goblet from an Egyptian tomb, and tell what Pharaoh drank out of it.

"But the work at the entrance was very recent," Monk muttered. "It hasn't been done over a week or two, I'll bet."

The steps ended. The tunnel traveled straight ahead for a few feet. It emptied then into what appeared to be a subterranean room.

Doc snapped a long, glaring white beam from his flashlight, and roved it slowly about.

"Holy cow!" breathed Renny in awe-stricken tones.

Chapter 18

THE SKELETON CREW

The underground recess was not as large as it had seemed at first. It was, in fact, hardly more than enough to contain the thing it held.

The walls to the right were solid and smooth—once a canyon side. To the left was rock—cracked, distorted slide-in rock, but solid for all of that.

A small rill of water crawled across the sandy floor. It looked like a flow of molten silver.

The galleon had bulked big in front of their eyes. It had been blocked up on rocks for a hull-scraping when disaster had overtaken it. The fact that it had been blocked up had preserved it from dampness to a certain extent. But it was not exactly seaworthy.

Once the galleon might have been a gilded pride of the Spanish Main. No telling what colors had bedecked it. But it was gray now—gray because of a repulsive mold which covered it like a carpet.

To the left of where Doc and his men stood, a skeleton lay on a rock. It lay in a curled position, like a slumbering dog. One of the hands, from which part of the finger bones had dropped, was over a gaping eye socket, as if to keep out the light.

"One of the galleon crew I guess," said Renny. The big engineer's enormous voice was a booming roar which assumed ear-splitting proportions in the cavern confines.

"Use your muffler!" Monk whispered. "You'll shake this place down on us."

Doc Savage turned. His flash beam, like a rod of white flame, impaled each of his men in turn. In their eagerness, all four had followed him into the tunnel.

The flash beam went to the sandy floor. Tracks were there. Fresh tracks! The imprints were those of moccasins!

Doc moved along the side of the galleon, his men trailing him. They passed three more skeletons. Rusty streaks beside the bone assemblies might once have been blunderbusses or swords.

Several piles of rust along the cavern wall hinted at cannons which must have been removed to lighten the galleon for careening.

Reaching out, Doc placed a finger against the hull. With a little pressure, the finger sank for half its length into the mold-covered wood. The galleon was a pile of rot.

Doc came to a halt. Before him in the hull of the galleon, a hole gaped. It was a fresh hole, and at least four feet square. It looked like it had been dug open with a spade.

Doc popped his light into the hole. There were more skeletons—five, six, seven of them, this time. They were gray things, made utterly hideous by the mold which covered them.

It was indeed a macabre argosy, this ship from another age, with its crew of skeletons.

Doc entered. He sank ankle-deep in the spongy timbers. It seemed inevitable that the whole ship would come down about his ears.

Going on, his light picked up objects which bore a marked resemblance to the brass-bound chests which historians write of. He dropped the glittering thread of light into one of these.

"Empty!" Renny thundered. "The treasure is gone!"

Doc Savage stepped swiftly to each of the chests in turn. He worked his way aft through a bulkhead. More of the chests were there. He picked up a small circular piece of metal and a green, glittering object which might have been colored glass—but wasn't.

He carried the articles back and showed them to his men.

"A piece-of-eight, and a small emerald!" Monk muttered. "That indicates there was really a treasure here."

Ham punched angrily at a bulkhead with his sword cane. The cane sank part of its length in the loggy wood.

"It's gone!" he snapped. "Who got it?"

"You noticed those tracks," Doc said. "They were made by feet shod in moccasins."

Ham frowned. "You mean—Boat Face?"

"Boat Face made the tracks," Doc said. "Not only did the Indian have the ivory cube, but he knew its significance. The gang who was after it must have told him what it was. Probably they hired him to get it for them. Then, when he double-crossed them, they killed him."

"It looks like our job now is to find out where Boat Face put the treasure," Renny grumbled.

"Maybe he didn't take it out of here," Monk offered. "After all, this is as good a hiding place as any. Let's look around."

Monk started for the stern. Doc was at his side. They passed through an aperture which had been spaded in a molded bulkhead.

Doc suddenly dropped a hand on Monk's shoulder. Monk's gristled, apish frame weighed in the neighborhood of two hundred and fifty pounds, but Doc's hand brought him up as sharply as if he had been a child.

"Back!" Doc rapped.

"Blazes! What's wrong?" Monk had wheeled, was diving back the way he had come as he asked the question.

Doc Savage made no answer. He was close behind Monk. Just before leaving the compartment, he halted, half turned, and popped his flashlight ahead.

The light disclosed a thin thread as gray as the mold which covered every inch of the ancient galleon. The thread was about six inches above the floor.

Wheeling, Doc followed Monk back to the others. They all stared at him, expecting an explanation. They were all a bit on edge. This place they were in—a grave which covered a hideous ship and its macabre crew of skeletons—had got under their skin somewhat.

Doc did not explain.

"Outside!" he said.

They scrambled into the rock tunnel, mounted the steps, and stumbled out into the night.

The cup-shaped depression into which the tunnel mouth opened was fairly deep. The moon was low in the sky. Its beams did not penetrate to the depression bottom.

"Whe-e-ew!" said Monk. "I'm glad to get out of that place! What went wrong, Doc?"

"Plenty has gone wrong—for you, amigos!" announced a guttural voice.

With that, several flashlights poked white funnels down over the depression rim. Doc and his men were wrapped in a white glare of light.

Squinting against glare, they could see men with guns on all sides of them.

One of the encircling gang hastily left his fellows and darted down the side of the depression. His gait down the steep slope was a series of grotesque hops. He came to a stop about halfway down.

"We know all about the gas!" said the guttural voice which had spoken previously. "I mean, Señor Savage, the gas which does its work while you hold your breath. Do not try to use it. If the man who just came near you drops, we will begin shooting. Sabe?"

Monk and Ham exchanged uneasy looks. They had forgotten their animosity. Johnny and Renny stood perfectly still.

Each of Doc's men carried one of the little supermachine guns under his coat. They debated their chances of seizing the guns and making a fight of it. The chances seemed slim.

"Easy does it," Doc said in an expressionless voice. "If we start fireworks, we haven't a chance."

"That is very sensible, hombres," said the voice above. "Each of you will remove his upper garments. Strip to the skin. Roll up your trousers legs to show no weapons are concealed beneath them. Turn your trousers pockets inside out."

The speaker was not one of the ring of gunmen. He stood behind them, hidden from view.

Doc and his four men stripped off coats, shirts, and undershirts. Doc shed his remarkable vest. They rolled up trousers legs, then turned pockets out.

"Bueno!" said the masked man. "We can now be sure that they have no weapons left. Go, amigos, and seize them!"

Men came sliding down the side of the depression.

Doc Savage had seen all of the gang on other occasions. They were the kidnapers of Patricia Savage. Doc counted eleven of them. That was the entire gang, except the leader.

Their chief did not appear. He remained above, unseen.

The men carried ropes. They began tying the prisoners. One fellow's rope was of extraordinary length, and it was he who bound Doc Savage.

The ropes were not of hemp, but of braided cotton. They were very strong. The men doing the knotting knew how it should be done.

Apparently, Doc submitted meekly to the binding. But a close observer might have noticed that the cables of muscles on his wrists were even larger than usual. Doc was holding the tendons tense. If he were tied while they were thus, he had merely to relax to get sufficient slack to shake off the binding ropes.

One of the swarthy gang had a canvas bag slung over a shoulder. From this, he drew a bottle-shaped object of shiny metal. The neck was fitted with a valve.

"Now, I will give the hombres the same thing I gave Alex Savage!" growled the man.

From the same sack, which had held the metal flask, the fellow withdrew two fragments of rather floppy rubber. These were carved, rubber-stamp fashion. The carving was that of a wolf with strangely human features. These were obviously the stamps used to leave the weird werewolf marks.

The gold flakes in Doc's eyes seemed to have turned to a tawny frost.

Here was the murderer of Alex Savage!

"No!" called the unseen leader from above. "Not the gas!"

"We can leave them somewhere," muttered the man with the gas flask. "No one can tell but what they died of heart failure."

"No! Not yet!"

Reluctantly, the swarthy man replaced the metal gas bottle in the canvas bag container.

Another dark man drew a knife. He juggled the blade in a way which showed remarkable dexterity. His manner indicated he was the knife-throwing expert of the group, and that he was proud of it.

"Then I will dispose of them as I did Boat Face, amigos," he smirked.

Doc Savage said nothing, made no move. It was a bad sign, the frank way these fellows were speaking of past crimes. It meant that they had little intention of Doc and his men living to bear witness—to tell a jury what they had heard.

"No!" said the concealed chief. "No knife—yet!"

The hidden leader now showed himself. He came skidding down the slope. He was a tall man; little more than that could be seen of him. He wore a mask—a great bandanna handkerchief which covered his head as well as his features.

Doc Savage glanced at Monk.

"Do you know this fellow, Monk?" he asked dryly.

Monk squinted at the masked man. "Nope. Can't recognize 'im."

"Isn't his walk familiar?"

Monk considered, acting as if the individual they were discussing were not present.

"Ain't able to tell, Doc," he said. "You'll have to spill it."

"O. K.," said Doc. "The bird is——"

The masked man snarled. He doubled and scooped up one of the tiny supermachine guns which Doc had been forced to drop. Leveling it, he shot Doc in his unprotected chest.

Chapter 19

THE KILLING DEAD

Doc dropped. The tiny machine gun happened to be latched into single-shot position. That was fortunate. Even though the gun was charged with mercy bullets, at that short range a flood of the slugs would have wrought fatal injury.

As it was, Doc took only one mercy bullet in the chest. The stupefying chemical worked swiftly. Doc was probably asleep before he hit the ground.

Monk and the others stared at their bronze chief. They were dazed. Now that they thought back, this was the first time they could remember having seen Doc entirely helpless.

They themselves, being bound with rope which was beyond their strength to break, were powerless to aid their bronze chief.

"Bueno!" said the swarthy man who wielded knives. "Let us give him another bullet—a real bullet!"

The masked man shook his head slowly. "No, amigos! We will delay that. These men may have removed the treasure. If so, we will have to make them lead us to it."

The fellow stepped into the tunnel, his followers crowding eagerly after him. They were hungry for sight of this loot which they had gone to such pains to get.

None troubled to watch the prisoners. They were bound too tightly to escape, it seemed.

The last man vanished into the tunnel.

Monk and the others wrenched at the ropes. They tried to untie each other's bonds with their teeth. The task was not hopeless, but it would take many minutes.

"We'll never make it!" Johnny groaned.

Repeatedly, the men glanced at Doc. They knew the bronze giant was a wizard as an escape artist. These ropes, as vigorously as they had been tied, would hardly hold Doc. But the metallic giant was a victim of the mercy bullet.

Or was he?

The swarthy men had left a flashlight stuck in the side of the depression. The beam of this played directly on Doc. The bronze man's lids seemed to flutter—they *did* flutter!

"Doc!" Renny rumbled softly.

Renny was incredulous. He knew the stupefying power of the mercy bullets; he had not believed a man could recover from their effects in less than thirty minutes.

Hardly ten minutes had elapsed since Doc collapsed. His recovery so soon was a tribute to his fine physical condition.

Doc lay perfectly motionless for a time. When finally he spoke, his voice was unexcited.

"Where did they go?"

"You mean the gang that grabbed us—and the masked big shot?" Monk asked.

"Yes."

"They went into the tunnel."

With a tremendous, convulsive effort, Doc gained his feet. The wound on his chest was small, merely a puncture which hardly oozed crimson.

"They'll be killed—at the galleon!" he rapped. "We may have time to get 'em out before——"

Doc's words were still banging through the surrounding night, when the earth seemed to heave several inches underfoot.

There was a tremendous, bellowing roar! It seemed to start deep in the earth, and gain and gain in volume. The ground vibrated as if it were about to fall to pieces! Boulders and gravel showered down the depression sides!

Out of the tunnel maw came a dragon-breath spout of crimson fire. A gush of yellow smoke followed it. Then the tunnel seemed to shut itself like a big mouth closing.

The quaking of the earth stopped; the rumbling died. A few rocks galloped the last of the distance down the slope. Then there was silence.

Renny used the exclamation he employed on such occasions.

"Holy cow!" he exploded. "What happened?"

Doc Savage did not answer immediately. Instead, he twisted his arms into various positions. The great muscles that had been tense when he was bound had relaxed now. The rope which had secured him fell away.

He started untying his friends, making explanations as he worked.

ιnere was a thread stretched across one of the galleon cabins," he said. "It ran to a contact that was barely visible at one side. The contact could have only one purpose—it was connected to an electric detonator for dynamite or gunpowder."

"So that's why you rushed us out of the galleon!" Monk exclaimed.

Doc nodded. "There was a chance of other contacts, better concealed, in other parts of the craft."

"Boat Face's work, huh?" Monk guessed. "But why'd he do it?"

"Boat Face evidently did it," Doc agreed. "He was the only visitor to the place before ourselves; his tracks prove that. He must have known he was mixed up with bad actors. Possibly he set the trap to get rid of them. He might have intended to give them the ivory block so that they would visit the galleon."

Monk stared at the tunnel which had closed like a mouth.

"Boat Face did a great job—for a dead man," he said. "They're all finished—down below."

Doc nodded. "No doubt of it."

Monk swung his gaze back to Doc. "Who was the masked guy, Doc?"

Doc started to answer, but held the words back when he heard a distant cry. The sound was shrilly feminine, cutting through the night. Patricia Savage's voice! She was anxious as to the fate of the men.

"They heard the explosion, and are worring about us!" Doc decided aloud, instead of answering Monk's question. "We'd better let them know we're safe."

Doc went to meet Patricia. He encountered her within two hundred yards. With the girl were Long Tom, ample Tiny, Señorita Oveja, and Señor Oveja.

Girl-faced El Rabanos was not with them.

Long Tom was excited.

"What happened?" he gulped.

"Where's El Rabanos?" Monk countered.

"Blasted if I know!" Long Tom retorted. "He disappeared, somehow, without me hearing him with the listening device. The only way he could have done it was to creep off at the same time you birds left—following you. Your noise covered his footsteps."

"That explains how the gang found us," Doc told Monk.

Monk emitted a long whistle. "So the guy in the mask was El Rabanos!"

"The master mind behind all this violence was El Rabanos," Doc agreed.

"Eso hace temblar!" Señor Oveja moaned.

El Rabanos—my best friend! A double-cross

"The same gentleman who ordered his men to
on the train—using my baggage straps," Doc agre
him credit for a devilish mind! He covered himself by
you think I was an enemy."

"But the treasure!" exclaimed Monk. "Where is it?"

Doc Savage turned to Patricia. "I showed you the sand
from Boat Face's moccasins," he said. "You said you knew of
a pool in a creek which had that kind of sand on its bottom.
You said you remembered wading there. You went to exam-
ine it. What did you find?"

"The treasure," Patricia said. "Boat Face had carried it out
and sunk it. The stuff was in fairly deep water. It was in
carrying it out to deep water that Boat Face got the sand in
his moccasins."

From a pocket, she produced a thin string of scintillating
color. It was a bangle of emeralds strung on gold.

"Here's a sample of the stuff."

Señor Oveja stared at the bauble. He suddenly forgot his
grief over his friend's treachery.

"I demand a share, amigos!" he said aggressively. "At least
three fourths of the treasure!"

Doc Savage ignored him.

"What disposition will be made of the treasure," Patricia
asked. Then, lest motives be misunderstood, she added: "I
don't want any."

"Nobody will get any," Doc said dryly. "Some of it came
from the churches of old Panama City. That portion should be
easily identified. It will be turned over to the church, its right-
ful owner."

He considered. "The rest will be used to build public hos-
pitals here in Canada, and to establish a trust fund to keep
them operating without charge to patients. That is what we
usually do with any money that comes our way."

"Wonder how much the stuff is worth?" Monk pondered.

"Several millions at least," Patricia said. "I know a little of
jewels—enough to guess at the value."

Señor Oveja waved his arms excitedly and shrieked: "But
what do I get out of it?"

"You," Doc told him, "get the air!"